NIGHT RAIDERS

OXFORD
UNIVERSITY PRESS

Great Clarendon Street, Oxford OX2 6DP

Oxford University Press is a department of the University of Oxford.
It furthers the University's objective of excellence in research, scholarship,
and education by publishing worldwide. Oxford is a registered trade mark of
Oxford University Press in the UK and in certain other countries

British Library Cataloguing in Publication Data
Data available

ISBN: 978-0-19-274996-3

1 3 5 7 9 10 8 6 4 2

Printed in Great Britain

Paper used in the production of this book is a natural,
recyclable product made from wood grown in sustainable forests.
The manufacturing process conforms to the environmental
regulations of the country of origin.

ALI SPARKES

NIGHT RAIDERS

OXFORD
UNIVERSITY PRESS

There was a sudden prickling sensation and a hissing sound. Matt and Tima shouted out and Elena spun around to see them patting against the inner curve of a pale lilac dome.

'The force field!' yelled Tima. 'It's back on!'

'That's right,' said Carra. 'It's back on. Nothing can get out and nothing can get in. Your insects can't reach me here, Tima, and your friends are about to find out the truth about you. I might be able to let them go—but you . . .' She gave a regretful sigh. 'I can't let you out alive.'

CHAPTER 1

It was Tima who found the body.

A frozen, pale thing like roadkill. Except human.

It wasn't the night out she was planning.

She'd got up at 1.34 a.m. as usual, thrown on her black jeans, jumper, and black leather jazz shoes, put her long dark hair into a neat side plait and left the house. All pretty standard.

Of course, it wasn't standard at *all*. The average eleven-year-old needs at least nine hours' sleep and Tima rarely got more than six. When the insomnia first started she had felt as if her life was disintegrating around her. These days, though, she seemed to have found a pattern; something workable.

She would go up to bed at nine, fall asleep by ten, wake up at 1.34 a.m. Meet up with Matt and Elena in the darker parts of the town. Get back to bed between 4.30 and 5 a.m. and maybe manage another one or two hours' sleep before getting up for school at seven. She was averaging five and a half hours' sleep most nights. About half what a girl her age should get. Hey-ho.

Elena was hanging upside down from one of the metal crossbeams under the conical roof of the bandstand, her dangling blonde ponytail gleaming in the moonlight. In the middle of the well-tended residents' gardens, the wood and wrought-iron structure had become a kind of clubhouse.

'Want a push?' Tima leapt up on to the wooden decking and gave Elena's shoulders a shove. Elena shrieked.

'Doooon't! I'm still working on this. I could fall!'

'You *won't* fall,' said Tima. Elena, in dark blue jeans, black trainers, and a black sweatshirt, was swinging by the crooks of her knees, like a gymnast on the high parallel bar. 'You're getting really fit!' Tima climbed up on to the balustrade that ran around three quarters of the bandstand. She grabbed a post, hauled herself up, hooked her knees over, and upended beside her friend. 'I have to say, though, I am *wondering* why you've got this obsession with hanging upside down . . . like a bat.'

'It's not an obsession,' said Elena. There was a defensive ring to her answer. 'I'm just trying to get fit. We need to be fit. We're out at night and we might meet a threat and—'

'Yeah, I know, it's OK,' cut in Tima, swinging easily; supple from years of dance-training. 'Still getting nightmares?'

Elena swung herself back and forth more energetically, then righted herself on the beam and dropped to the decking. 'I'm not worried about that,' she said. 'Nights are easy.' She picked up her small backpack and slung it over her shoulders before ambling out across the gardens towards the woods that bordered them.

Tima followed. She was about to ask how things were at home . . . but then spotted a familiar shape in the shadows.

'Look,' she said, smiling, 'someone's here to see you.'

Elena's face broke into a delighted beam and she dropped to her knees beside an old oak tree. A young vixen waited there; her three long-legged cubs, close to adulthood, playing nearby. Elena held out her hands and the animal moved fluidly into her embrace. The fox cubs followed their mother, gently mobbing their human friend, nibbling at her jeans and sweatshirt and playing tug of war with the straps that hung off her backpack.

Tima stood back and watched, smiling. She could join in any time she liked; the foxes were her friends too—but to Elena, they were like family. Tima's thoughts wandered to her own family . . . not Mum and Dad, back home, asleep, but the creatures that she connected most strongly with. Her Night Speaker family. True, they weren't as cuddly as Elena's Night Speaker family, but they were still pretty amazing.

She stepped away towards a clearing where the long grass was damp with overnight dew and glistening in the blue-white light of the moon. She gave the grass a little wave and at once a sparkling storm of wings rose from it. Tima grinned and then couldn't help laughing. 'Oh, you poor, daft things,' she said. Of all the insects she had grown to love over the summer, the humble crane fly was the most pitiable. With those wonky, trailing daddy-long-legs limbs, its flight was far from graceful. It had no working mouth parts—so it had no hope of a nice snack beyond a tiny sip of nectar. After months underground each crane fly was counting out its life in hours—days at best; most likely to end up as bird food before it even had a chance to mate. Yet still, here they all were, trying to dance for her.

If she'd walked into a cloud of crane flies this time last year, she would have screamed herself stupid. Now, though, she moved slowly through them, scores of ungainly legs and spindly wings brushing against her arms and face, and felt only fondness.

Then her foot struck something in the long grass. A dark mass lay half-hidden by the weeds and some sprawling runners of a blackberry-laden bramble bush. It was heavy and still and she could see a booted foot.

Oh God. A body.

'ELENA!' she screamed, as the crane flies scattered around her.

Elena was at her side seconds later.

'I don't want to look,' whimpered Tima, clapping her hands to her mouth. 'I don't want to see it.'

Elena knelt down and touched the body.

'Is it cold?' breathed Tima, through her fingers, her heart speeding up and her throat closing with dread.

Elena nodded, getting her torch out and flicking it on.

'Don't—don't roll it over,' begged Tima. 'We should just call the police or ambulance or something.'

Elena glanced up at her, a wry expression on her face. 'And then explain what we were doing out in the woods at two in the morning?' She rolled the body over. Tima squeezed her eyes shut. She didn't want to look into the face of a dead person.

Then she heard Elena gasp.

'*Spin!*'

Tima blinked open and stared in horror as Elena gently pulled the body on to its back. A familiar pale face gleamed in the moonlight, eyes shut, spiky white-blond hair squashed flat on one side and darkened with what looked like blood. 'Oh no,' Tima moaned. 'Is he dead?'

Elena put her fingers to the boy's throat, her mouth a tight line. Then she took a sudden breath and looked up. 'He's alive. I can feel a pulse.' She was pulling out her mobile phone with her spare hand.

'So *now* you're calling?' said Tima.

Elena's eyes flashed. 'He needs help!' She leant close in towards him, wiping some grass from his cheek. 'Spin! Spin! Can you hear me?' The boy did not move. Tima couldn't believe Elena had found a pulse. He had always been pale but now he was like stone. He looked really, *really* dead.

'Is he breathing?' Tima whispered, kneeling down next to Elena.

Elena put her face close to his, checking for any warmth. 'I . . . think so . . .' she said and then she shrieked as she was suddenly smashed backwards into the long grass.

Spin shot to his feet and struck out at Tima too, swiping her across the face so she was whacked sideways, the hot scent of blood suddenly pinging through her nose and throat.

'What the—?!' Elena struggled to a sitting position as the boy loomed over them both, his silky black trench coat billowing in the air behind him. Spin stared all around him and then hissed like an angry cat. His eyes were gleaming silver and what could only be described as *fangs* were clearly visible in his snarling mouth.

Elena scrambled to her feet, gasping, and then fell on to her backside as there was a sudden punch in the air and a cloud of grey smoke erupted where Spin had been standing. When it cleared . . . he was gone.

Tima, holding her left cheek, let out a long, shaky breath and glanced across at Elena. 'Still want to impress your vampire boyfriend *now*?'

CHAPTER 2

'What the hell happened to *you*?' Matt flashed his torch in a wide beam across Tima's face and then across to Elena's.

'*Spin* happened to us,' muttered Tima, lightly touching the scratch across her cheek.

'It's stopped bleeding now,' said Elena. 'It's not deep.' She sat down on a crate next to the barn and leant her back up against the old wooden wall. She closed her eyes as Tima told Matt about what had happened.

Matt was furious. A wide selection of names for Spin spilt out of him in an angry torrent—not one of them suitable for an eleven-year-old to hear. But Tima wasn't your average eleven-year-old—any more than Elena was an average fourteen or Matt an average fifteen. With a sigh, Elena pressed her fingertips across the swelling on her forehead. It was painful. She shuddered to think what the bruise would look like tomorrow.

'He *headbutted* Elena?' Matt was raging. 'I'm going to break his face.'

'It wasn't deliberate,' Elena said. 'He was . . . freaked out. He'd been unconscious. We thought he was *dead*.'

'Yeah? Or maybe that was just another one of his little fun tricks,' snapped Matt. 'Play dead until you get up close and then attack. You fell for it.'

'*Why* would he want to attack us?' argued Elena.

Tima slid into the old tyre swing and began to rock to and fro in it. 'Who can tell? He's not normal.'

'Yeah, well,' muttered Elena. 'You're a girl who commands insects. That's not normal, either.'

Matt's dark eyes glinted dangerously. He reached into his backpack and pulled out a stout wooden rounders bat. 'Next time I see him, I'm going to teach him a lesson.'

Elena felt alarm flare through her, making her forehead throb. 'Matt . . . please—just don't mess with him. You know how fast he is. He could beat all three of us at once. Let's . . . just steer clear of him. He hasn't bothered us for ages and I really don't think tonight was some kind of trap. He was cold . . . cold as stone. Something happened to him.'

'Yeah, well, if you believe all this vampire stuff, he *would* be cold, wouldn't he? Maybe I should sharpen the end of this,' he shook the bat, 'and stake him through the heart.'

Tima slowed on her tyre swing. 'The eyes and the fangs and the smoke . . . they did look really . . .'

'OK—enough of this,' said Elena. 'Spin is just . . . Spin. And we don't need to have anything to do with him. And actually, Matt—I don't think it's Spin you're really so angry about, is it?' She got up, grabbed his torch and played the light across *his* face. There was a long red graze down one side of it. 'That doesn't look like your dad's work. Has Liam's gang been chasing you again?'

Matt grabbed the torch back and growled: 'It's nothing to do with you. I can handle it. I *did* handle it.'

Tima jumped off the tyre swing and wrapped her arms around Matt, peering up at his wounded face. 'Oh Matt—it's horrible. What happened?'

Matt and Elena glanced at each other, bemused. Tima was quite a hugger and they still hadn't got used to it. Matt rolled his eyes and shrugged away from her. He sat down on a pile of logs and pulled a bit of folded paper out of his jeans pocket. 'It was my own stupid fault. I had to go and win something.'

'*Win* something?' echoed Elena, reaching for the paper. 'Win what?'

'The Year Ten writing competition,' he muttered, looking at his feet.

Elena stared at him for a few seconds. Matt winning a writing competition? A few months ago the only competition he would have won was Bruiser of the Year. 'Wow,' she said.

'Yeah, wow,' he echoed. 'I don't know what came over me. I wrote this story called "God of Dark Light".'

'O . . . K,' said Elena. She and Tima exchanged glances.

'Anyway, I thought it was just, you know, rubbish. But it

won. They called me up to get a book token in assembly.'

Tima asked: 'Why was that a problem? That's a brilliant thing!'

'Oh yeah, brilliant,' grunted Matt. 'Liam Bassiter and his mates were so impressed they decided to beat me up on the way home from school by way of congratulations.'

'Ouch,' said Tima. 'So glad I don't go to your school.'

'Yeah well, *they* said ouch too,' muttered Matt. 'You should see *their* faces. I could take any one of them any day. Just not three of them at once . . . Just as well Lucky wasn't there. She'd have taken their eyes out.'

Elena felt her shoulders stiffen. Matt's starling was fiercely protective of him; who knew what the bird might do if he didn't stop her? 'You know you can't ever let her . . . don't you, Matt? Or any of her friends . . . you know you can't let them attack.'

Matt nodded and looked away.

'Wait . . .' Elena stepped around him and stared into his face. 'What happened?'

'Nothing,' he said, still avoiding her gaze.

'No. Something. What?'

'Well, there were some gulls about. We were near the dump.'

'You didn't!' Elena stared at him. 'You didn't let them attack.'

'NO! I just let them . . . drop some cack. A lot of it.'

Tima gave a shout of laughter and Matt grinned. 'They were blinded by cack,' he said, snorting. 'Long enough for me to walk away.'

Elena heaved a sigh of relief. 'OK. Good . . . but even so—'

'Yeah, yeah, I know what you're going to say!' said Matt.

'How does it go? *With great power comes great responsibility . . .*'

'Well, that's Uncle Ben in *Spider-Man*,' said Elena. 'But . . . yeah. I guess so.'

'*You wouldn't like me when I'm angry*,' growled Tima. Matt and Elena laughed—it sounded so funny coming from the petite, pretty girl. 'The Incredible Hulk,' added Tima, with a nod. 'I know! We need a Night Speakers warning catchphrase. How about,' she dropped into another growl: '*Don't make me set my moths on you . . . ?*'

Matt joined in with a comedy snarl: '*Push me—get pecked to death*.'

Elena paused to think and then supplied: '*Fight me—fight my foxes.*'

Matt and Tima pursed their lips. Elena sighed. 'All right—it's a work in progress. Anyway—all I'm saying is . . . we can't let people know that we have this . . . *thing* . . . with animals. We don't need the attention, do we? If people start noticing us, we won't be free. And I'd hate that. I'd hate to lose . . .' she glanced around at the sweet welcoming night that had come to mean so much to her, '. . . this.'

'Oh yeah . . . talking of "this",' said Matt. 'There's a little owl across the field I want you to meet. He's got a face like serial killer.'

'He *is* a serial killer,' observed Tima. 'If you're a vole.' They headed across the sea of shifting, whispering wheat.

'Yeah—the night is full of killers,' agreed Matt.

CHAPTER 3

Tima peered at the long scratch on her left cheek in the bathroom mirror. It wasn't bleeding now but it positively *glowed* red. How was she going to get *this* past Mum and Dad? When they'd kissed her goodnight around 9 p.m. her skin had been clear and undamaged—now it looked like she'd been in a scrap with a cat.

Hmmm. Next door had a cat. OK . . . she leant her forehead against the mirror, working out her story. She would say she'd nipped out into the garden first thing . . . to . . . er . . . *what?* Why would she go out before her mum and dad were even up? Um . . . she'd left something out there. Her mobile phone . . . on the garden seat. Yes. That would do it. She'd woken up to realize it was missing and remembered where she'd left it. So she'd nipped out and she'd met next door's cat, played with it, and got a scratch.

Tima shook her head as she switched off the bathroom light. It wasn't in her nature to lie to her parents. Her life had never been this complicated back when she was normal. But since May, since the waking up started, life had got very complicated. Amazing. But complicated.

She wandered through the dark landing, back into her bedroom. It was 5.15 a.m. and it wouldn't be light until around six. At 1.34 a.m. the beam had shot through her bedroom as it did every night at exactly the same time. It was only there for a few seconds and it always woke her up, but sometimes, these days, she woke up a few minutes beforehand and waited for it. Watched and listened for it, nerves tingling with anticipation. The beam was barely visible but when she caught a glimpse it was like a thin stream of gold, filled with curls and bubbles. The song it sang was just as beautiful—distant and sweet and mysterious, like a carol from the stars. It chased through her world for a few seconds every twenty-four hours and then vanished, always leaving her dazed and thrilled.

What if she woke up one night and the beam did *not* come through?

She would miss it. Terribly. OK, it had totally messed up her life and made her an insomniac—but it had also made her a Night Speaker. It had made her run out into the dark and find Elena and Matt; discover that they too were waking at the same time; find out that the same beam intersected each of their homes on a straight line. The three were connected for ever now because they alone saw and heard and felt the beam. And they

13

alone—as far as they knew—could communicate fluently with the animal world.

Through a gap in her curtains she saw movement . . . someone across the other side of the road. *Not Spin again*, was her first thought. But no. Someone *was* there, though. A girl or a young woman was in the grass across the way, on the edge of the path that led down to the residents' gardens and the bandstand. She was crouched over on her hands and knees. Why?

Tima turned and ran silently down the stairs, opened the front door without a squeak (she had secretly oiled the hinges weeks ago) and leapt over the front wall. She walked across the empty road, glancing at the luminous eastern sky, and stood by the stranger. 'What have you lost?' she said.

A surprised face tilted up to her; a woman, perhaps in her mid-twenties. Her hair was long and dark and she was dressed in something a bit like biker gear; lots of dark green leather. She was also struggling to breathe.

'My—my inhaler,' she said. 'I dropped it somewhere around here.' Her accent was hard to place. It was clipped and rather too perfect. *Scandinavian?* Tima wondered. Difficult to tell when her breathing was so laboured.

'Let me help you,' said Tima, kneeling down. She didn't start rummaging around in the grass, though. She just sent a message to the ants and asked them to pass it along. She'd seen inhalers before—a girl at school used one for her asthma. It was blue and L-shaped with a little metal canister inside it. She sent the image to the insects and asked them to find it.

In the corner of her eye she saw a small pillar of specks rise

14

up a metre or so away from where the woman was searching: some gnats hovering above the grass. She crawled across, put her hand into the damp vegetation, and pulled out something small and metallic. *Thanks*, she sent, as the gnats scattered. It didn't look much like the inhalers she'd seen before—it was silver for a start, and was canister-shaped with a kind of tiny fan in one end. 'Is this it?' she said.

The woman turned from her own search. 'Oh yes! Thank you!' She took the silver thing, flipped a cap off the base of it, tipped her chin up as if she was going to do some sword-swallowing, and took a deep breath through the inhaler. It made a slightly comical whizzing sound.

'Oh, thank the green mountains!' murmured the woman, letting out a long sigh of relief. 'That is better.' The wheezing had stopped.

'Green mountains probably wouldn't help . . .' said Tima. '. . . if you're allergic to mountain ash trees. I've got a friend at school who's allergic to mountain ash trees. They make her wheeze. Are you OK now?' She stood up, getting edgy now that dawn was so close. Dad would be up any time now. He had an early shift at the hospital.

'Wait,' said the woman, getting to her feet. She was tall and slender and rather beautiful, with eyes that lifted up a little at the edges. 'May I ask you something?' the woman said, tilting her head sharply, like Lucky.

Tima expected her to add: 'What's a kid like you doing out alone in the dark?' but instead she said: 'Where are the nurseries?'

Tima blinked. 'The nurseries?'

'Yes—the nurseries. The . . . er . . . places where things are grown from small.'

Tima wrinkled her brow. 'Small things? Do you mean plants or children?'

'Children?' Now the woman looked baffled. She must be Scandinavian, Tima decided. She obviously didn't understand quite everything in English.

'Well, preschools and kindergartens are known as nurseries too,' Tima explained. 'And we also call garden centres, where plants and seedlings are grown, nurseries. Which type do you mean?'

The woman nodded, eyebrows raised. 'I see. Seedlings. Please. Where are the seedlings grown?'

'Well . . . my parents go to one over in Hazleton—it's about half an hour's drive from here. They get plants and stuff from there. And there's a garden centre place up at Cranmere House—you know, the stately home. You can look it all up online—find out exactly where they are.'

'Online,' repeated the woman, thoughtfully. 'OK. Thank you.' And she turned sharply and walked away into the trees.

Tima watched her go, bemused. Then pale shafts of gold began to reach over the eastern horizon and she hurried back into the house, ran upstairs on tiptoes, and skidded into her bedroom literally seconds before Dad wandered out on to the landing, heading for his wake-up shower.

*

In the woods the woman collected her backpack from a tree, high up on a branch where she'd been sleeping earlier, and checked her weaponry. She could breathe well again but something else was making her heart race a little too fast and it wasn't the Thornleigh air or the drugs from her inhaler. Of all the things she had been prepared for, on arriving here, she had *never* expected this. How could that girl possibly have understood her words, when she had sent up her casual thanks to the green mountains? Not only was it a phrase never, to her certain knowledge, used here—she'd uttered it, in a moment of lapse, in her own language.

And that girl could not *possibly* have ever heard that language before.

CHAPTER 4

HARCOURT HIGH ACADEMY TIMETABLE FOR: *Matteus Wheeler*	DAY: *Tuesday*	LOCATION:
8.30 a.m. REGISTRATION		TUTOR GROUP V9
8.50—9.40 a.m.	Physics	C Block Class 5
9.45—10.55 a.m.	Physics	C Block Class 5
BREAK	Get head kicked in	Behind kitchen bins
11.10—midday	English	A Block Class 3
12.10—1 p.m.	Maths	C Block Class 1
LUNCH BREAK	Smash Liam in the mouth, punch Ahmed in the gut, get head kicked in again, wreck marrows and melons	Edge of school field
1.30—2.20 p.m	History	A Block Class 1
2.20—3 p.m.	Get punishment	Head teacher's office

'What disappoints me most,' said Mr Rosen, 'is that you *seemed* to be getting past all the fighting and time wasting. I really thought, after all that happened to you last term, you'd turned over a new leaf.' He absent-mindedly stroked a leaf as he said it—one of the many that were crowded on a shelf in his room. Mr Rosen had a thing for plants. As soon as he'd arrived at the school last spring he'd filled his office with leafy friends which he tended carefully. Even the greenery in his fish tank was in top-notch condition.

Matt stared down at his scuffed school shoes and stained trousers and silently raged. He *had* been turning over a new leaf. He *was* past all the fighting and time wasting. And then Liam Bassiter showed up.

'Your teachers tell me that you have actually been improving in recent months,' went on Mr Rosen, breaking off from the plant tickling to go and gaze through the high, metal-framed window down to the school field and the woods beyond it. 'We really thought that after your accident and your short stay in hospital back in May, you'd had a life-changing experience.'

Well, you're right about THAT, thought Matt. *Battling with an underworld god intent on slaughtering your entire home town will do that for you. No, really, don't thank me.*

'And now poor Mr Janssen has had to deal with you stamping through the school garden, fighting, swearing, destroying his work. I'm so disappointed in you.'

Poor Mr Janssen? Mr Janssen was built like a bear and had smashed Matt and Liam's heads together when they'd stumbled into his poxy marrow patch. Matt was pretty sure they'd both got a light concussion.

Of course, he'd known it was coming. After the gulls incident yesterday, killing himself laughing as they staggered about, wiping bird muck out of their eyes, there was no way this was over. Liam, Ahmed, and Tyler were looking daggers at him in registration. In Physics they were kicking the back of his seat and muttering death threats. In break they—and two more hangers-on—followed him closely out of class and he, knowing what was coming, headed for the library, only to find it was closed for some kind of restocking.

'Oh *no*—can't hide behind your books today?' sneered Liam.

Matt walked past him, deliberately smashing his shoulder into Liam's. 'Nice hair doodles,' he said, glancing back at the elaborate carvings in Liam's ginger buzz-cut. 'Does your mum do them for you?'

They followed so close they were stepping on his heels and shoving at his backpack, scanning at all times for teachers. Matt left the building and walked towards the music block. He wasn't scared; he was angry—and ready. He could take Liam any day of the week—and soon he was proving it in the concrete courtyard behind the bins. The rest of them stood watching, a thrilled audience whooping in whispers, careful not to attract a teacher. Just weeks ago these had been his mates.

Matt got some good blows in and had the satisfaction of hearing Liam shriek in pain as he seized his arm, mid-throw, and twisted it up behind his back. But then they all bundled in—five on one. He got a good punch to Ahmed's traitorous belly before going down, and then he was on the floor, jammed against one of the heavy metal bins, taking kicks to the head. The bell rang and his attackers abruptly stopped and walked away, laughing. The whole thing, start to finish, had lasted less than a minute.

He lay still for a moment, then dusted himself off, went for a quick wash in the boys' toilets and on to A Block for English. None of them were in that class—he had been bumped up to the top set after his writing got stupidly award-winning. Nobody paid him any attention in English and then it was lunchtime and round two.

This time he was stalked through the dining hall, where he ate his lunch while Liam's gang threw chips at him whenever the canteen staff weren't looking. When he got up to go outside he felt like the Pied Piper, with six boys now trailing in his wake, excited and ready for action. Within seconds of heading down on to the school field they were upon him, ripping his pack off his back, emptying it into the grass, throwing his wildlife and bird books from the library at him.

He didn't remember even *thinking* about Lucky. She often waited for him up on a lamp post as he left school but she must have been in the area early. Because, as he lay on his back, wrestling with Liam and getting kicks from the others, a dark cloud formed in the sky above them. Glancing up, Matt realized it was a massive murmuration of starlings. He tried to shout 'NO!' at Lucky, because he knew she was among them, leading them. But Liam got in a punch to his belly at that moment and drove the wind out of him.

Then the birds descended.

They went for the whole group, dive-bombing with beaks and claws, sending the boys scattering and shrieking, before Matt got enough breath back to shout: 'NO! Lucky, STOP!'

The murmuration ceased and swooped up again but a dozen starlings were still attacking Liam. He ran across the field towards the school's new kitchen garden, a squawking flock around his head.

Matt chased after him, yelling at Lucky to stop.

Eventually she did, taking the other starlings with her into the trees.

Liam turned, red scratches on his face, and launched himself at Matt. Together they stumbled straight through the fine netting the school groundsman had set up. They landed in the marrows. Green and white mush splattered all around them and then they rolled across a polytunnel, flattening some leafy greens before smashing into some melons; more carnage followed with spatters of pink and red. It looked like a scene from a low-budget horror movie.

Mr Janssen was weeding in the far corner. He rose up with a roar of fury and charged at them like an angry bull. Grabbing them both by the back of the neck he lifted them up almost off their feet and dashed their heads together, shouting in rage: 'YOU DO NOT COME HERE! YOU DO *NOT* COME HERE!' His accent made him sound like the Terminator as he dragged them back across the school field, ranting furiously all the way. He did not let go of either of them until they were outside the head teacher's office.

'Your mother and father will be disappointed too,' went on

Mr Rosen, scratching at his greying dark hair and turning back from the window.

Matt snapped his attention back to the here and now. 'My father? You're going to tell him?'

Mr Rosen paused and tilted his head to one side. 'Matteus—I can't suspend you from school *without* letting your father know, can I?'

Matt felt panic rise in him. And fury. This was NOT his FAULT. He had been defending himself against attack. He had not gone looking for a fight. Over many years at school he *had* been in lots of fights and not once had he ever spoken a word about it when hauled up in front of the head teacher. He did not whine and blame. He didn't grass. That was not his way. But now . . . if his dad was told . . . things were going to be far worse for him at home than they had been behind the school bins and in the marrow patch.

Matt compressed his lips and stared past Mr Rosen to the sky outside. He should have called Lucky and her flock in *before* the fight had got started. Let them scare Liam off. He could have saved himself from all this. What was the point of his Night Speaker superpowers if he couldn't use them? Typical of Elena to go off on one about 'responsibility'. He jumped, startled, when Mr Rosen suddenly put a hand on his shoulder.

'Matt,' he said, in a gentler voice. 'I'm not an idiot. Mr Janssen told me it was five or six against one, but I could probably have worked that out. It's no secret things have been turbulent with you and your . . . old friends. Why don't you tell me what happened?'

Matt shook his head and looked back at the melon slush on his trousers. 'I'm sorry about the garden,' he said. 'I'll help to fix it if Mr Janssen wants me to. Just . . . please don't suspend me. And please don't tell my dad.'

Mr Rosen dropped his hand and sat back on the edge of his battered oak desk. 'What will happen if your dad finds out, Matt?'

'Nothing,' said Matt. Too quickly.

Mr Rosen's sharp eyes closed briefly behind his glasses and he rubbed his beaky nose for a few seconds. Then he said: 'My dad used to beat seven bells of hell out of me when I was a kid.'

Matt remained silent.

'I left home at sixteen to get away from him.'

Matt gulped.

'Is that what you'll do, Matt?'

'I'm joining the navy.'

Mr Rosen sighed and nodded. 'A fine career. But finer still if you go in at officer level, with some good GCSEs and A Levels.'

Matt gulped again. The trouble with the scant five hours of sleep he now got every night was that it made him weak. Emotional. He hadn't wanted to cry when he was getting kicked in the head. Why did he feel like crying now? He stared hard at the tropical fish; little glowing blue, red, and orange life forces, darting about in lime-green waterweed. As he focused on them, they all began to cluster in the closest corner of the tank, staring right back at him. He snapped his attention away from them.

'Matt—I'm going to offer you a deal,' said the head teacher. 'I *should* fill out a school incident form and send it to your parents right away. But I think that form could possibly get lost on my very messy desk . . . *if* you get past this business today and find a way to *stay* past it. Keep your head down. Keep going to the library and studying. It's not too late to aim for college and even university. You just need to stay out of trouble.'

'Thank you, sir,' said Matt, his cheeks hot and his voice croaky.

'And yes, I think you *should* go and help Mr Janssen repair the garden,' added the head teacher. 'And don't worry—I won't be sending Liam and Co. along with you. Liam *will* be getting a two-week suspension, along with the rest of them. I hope that will give you a bit of peace—and time to get yourself together.'

'Thank you, sir,' said Matt, again. He managed to look the man in the eye, too.

'OK—go on home now. And stay out of trouble.'

Lucky was on his shoulder five seconds after he exited the school gates. Matt reached up and stroked her shiny black head and she rubbed her beak against his fingers, making small chirruping sounds. Matt sniffed hard and headed home for his next shift at Kowski Kar Kleen. He really needed to toughen up.

CHAPTER 5

Spin lay in his dark cocoon, brooding. He did a good line in brooding. Had he been able to see himself in the mirror, he'd appreciate just how classically broody he could look. Lean face; high cheekbones catching the light and the shadow at just the right angle, white-blond hair tousled a little over his brow, mouth a straight, mean line despite its chiselled upper lip; blue-green eyes burning dark and dangerous.

His encounter with the woman had made a mark. A *sticky* mark. She had shot him in the face with some kind of *glue* pellet. He'd known next to nothing about it; just a stinging impact and then blackout. What was it? Some kind of paintball gun?

He'd been minding his own business when she'd shown up. He was perfectly innocently messing with a drunken idiot, just getting his fangs out, when there was a polite cough.

Spin paused. It was coming from behind him.

He saw hope of rescue in the drunken idiot's glassy eyes.

Another cough. Spin dumped his prey in a privet hedge and spun around on one black boot. A woman stood there. She was dressed in a dark-green leather jacket, matching trousers, and knee-high black boots, a thick belt buckled around her slender waist. She was unreasonably beautiful, with long black hair and dark eyes.

'Are you two finished?' she asked.

Spin turned to see his prey staggering down the road. He sighed. 'Looks like it.' He turned back, curiosity overtaking his annoyance, and made an ironic bow. 'How can I help?'

'Do you live around here?' she'd asked, hoisting a shiny black bag over one shoulder.

Spin considered. 'Depends what you mean by *live*,' he said.

'I'm not from around here.' She glanced up at the moon, shining through some cloud. 'I need some guidance from a friendly local.'

He gave a short cackle. 'Do I *look* friendly?'

She rolled her eyes. 'Everyone else I've encountered has been drunk or stupid. Please, can you list every nursery in this town and beyond it within a ten-mile radius?'

'Or maybe, I could just *bite you* instead?' he said, with a shrug.

'Can you help me?' she said, now getting something out of the bag. 'Or have I made a mistake?'

He let his eyes gleam up again—and inched the fangs out. He couldn't stop himself. He stepped closer too.

She sighed.

And shot him in the face.

That was the last he knew until the Insomnia Twins woke him up.

Damn! Back in his lair, a creeping, prickly feeling was riding across his shoulders and throat now. Was that . . . could it be . . . embarrassment? To be found by *them* in a state like *that*! This was *not* his style. He *always* had the upper hand. Almost always.

This time he'd been shot in the face, and then, judging by where he'd woken up, dragged some distance and dumped under a hedge. Then as soon as he'd come to, he'd headbutted Good Girl and swiped at Tiny Dancer before he even knew who they were. Of course, he'd had no idea it wasn't still that woman on her mission to find local nurseries. What was she? A lost childminder?

Tonight he'd get out and find her, if she was still around. Find her and disarm her and get some answers.

CHAPTER 6

'Keep still!'

Elena pulled Matt's chin up and peered at his face from different angles. In the mirror on the wall behind her he could see his left eye was a little puffed-up on one side and a dark red bruise on his cheekbone was getting more purple by the minute. A deep scratch on the right corner of his mouth was sticky with blood but not actually dripping.

'Look—can you make it better or what?' Matt said, through gritted teeth.

'I can clean it up but there's no way your dad's going to miss this,' said Elena. 'He's going to know.'

Matt blew out a frustrated breath. He wondered how many other boys in his year would get a good beating at home for getting a good beating at school. Dad would rage about him misbehaving and then teach him a good lesson on how to misbehave—as a reward for his misbehaviour. It was good news that Mr Rosen wasn't going to suspend him or contact his parents this once—but Dad would still have plenty of clues about what had happened today.

He thumped his fists on the kitchen table and growled.

Elena went to the fridge and pulled out a couple of cans of lemonade, plonked one down on the scratched pine table in front of him, cracked the ring pull with a hiss, and said: 'Drink.'

He did, finding comfort in the sugar and the bubbles and the fact that someone cared. Actually, after the unexpected turn of events in the head teacher's office, it seemed that *two* people cared.

'There's a chance they didn't make the connection,' Elena went on, taking a sip from her own can. 'Between you and the starlings. I mean . . . it could have been a coincidence.'

Matt shook his head. 'It stopped when I shouted STOP.'

'OK . . .' Elena shrugged. 'But they were all making a lot of noise. They might not have heard you. And anyway . . . who's ever going to believe them?'

'I thought you were going to give me the Spider-Man lecture,' he muttered.

Elena sighed. 'It wasn't your fault. You didn't *ask* the birds to help, did you?'

He shook his head glumly, sipped some more lemonade and leant back in the wooden chair. At once he winced and sat upright again. Elena paused in mid can-tilt and put the drink back down. She stood and walked around to him. 'Matt . . .

30

show me.' He shook his head. 'Come on. Stand up—show me.'
She pointed to his muddy school shirt.

He knew she wasn't going to give up, so he got to his feet
and eased his shirt up. Looking down, he understood why
Elena sucked in her breath. His torso looked like a flower show
exhibit; dark red roses blooming all around it.

'*How* many of them?' she asked.

He shrugged. 'Five or six.'

'Matt—I think you should get this looked at. I mean . . .
maybe you've broken a rib. This is . . . this is bad. It's *assault*. You
should go to the police.'

'Yeah, right,' said Matt. 'Because my dad would have no
problem with that.' He raised a grazed hand. 'It's fine. I can
handle it. It's only bruises. I just don't want to give him an
excuse to add any more.'

'Would he really? Would he do that?' Her round blue eyes
were wide, appalled. The shame that trickled through him was
worse than the pain.

'He might.'

'But *why*? It wasn't your fault! If you told him what
happened . . .'

'Look—it's two things, OK. One—he thinks he has to keep
control. If I'm scrapping with boys at school and getting into
trouble, it reflects on him—that he's not in control of me. That's
one thing.'

'And the other?'

'He's disappointed that I've not made a better job of it.
Haven't won.'

Elena sank back down on to her seat and he pulled his shirt down and sat opposite again, lifting the can and making a little ironic 'cheers' movement which she did not return.

'Well,' said Elena, suddenly determined. 'We can at least keep him from knowing for a day or two—until the bruises settle down. I'm going to need help from Mum though.'

'Your *mum*?' Matt glanced out into the back garden where Mrs Hickson was feverishly digging. 'I thought you said she's ill.'

'She is,' said Elena. 'She's a bit better since they tried her on some new meds, but she's still pretty manic. She has to have a project or she goes *really* manic. So I said we should have a garden pond.' She flicked her eyes guiltily across to the window. 'I knew it would take her ages to dig it and really tire her out. But—she can help us. She's brilliant at make-up.'

'Make-up?!' Matt twitched.

'Yes—proper stage make-up. Prosthetic make-up. She used to work in theatres. She's a costumier. And she knows make-up. She's got loads of it upstairs.'

'But—' said Matt, too late. Elena was already leaning out of the kitchen door.

'Mum!' she said. 'We need your help!'

Mrs Hickson arrived in the kitchen seconds later, wiping sweat and mud off her brow. She was an attractive woman with fair hair, a little wilder than her daughter's, and the same blue eyes. 'Hi Matt,' she said, grinning and puffing a little from her exertion with the spade. 'Oooh dear—what happened to *you*?'

'He got into a fight at school,' said Elena. 'And he'll be in real trouble when he gets home, looking like that—and it wasn't

32

his fault. So . . . can you do your thing with the make-up? Make him look a bit more normal?'

'It's all right, Mrs Hickson,' said Matt, getting up. 'You don't have to. It'll be fine.'

'Oooh, no you don't,' said Mrs Hickson, rushing to the sink and washing her hands. 'Sit down. I haven't had a chance to do anyone's face in *ages*. And call me Callie. Mrs Hickson sounds like an elderly postmistress.'

'Oh . . . OK . . . Callie,' said Matt. He sent a despairing look at Elena but she just grinned back at him and put both thumbs up.

Minutes later he was sitting obediently still while Callie raided a vast toolbox filled with make-up. She squirted something she called foundation on to his wrist, trying out several different shades until she was satisfied. Then she went to work, at speed, first cleaning and then gently smoothing some cool, translucent gel across the deep scratch at the corner of his mouth. 'Leave that to dry for a few minutes,' she muttered, totally absorbed. Then she applied the skin-coloured paint all over his bruises. After a few minutes of deft brushwork, she concentrated even finer efforts on the gelled-over scratch—and then applied a fine layer of silky powder to all of her work. Finally she stood back, checked his face on both sides, and nodded, proudly. 'You'll do.'

Matt fully expected to look ridiculous but as he turned to the mirror he was surprised to see . . . nothing. He looked *normal*. He got up, trying not to wince at the pain in his torso, and went closer to the mirror, open-mouthed, turning his head

33

to examine his face from all angles. 'Wow. That is—brilliant!'

Callie smiled and gave a little mock curtsy. 'We aim to please. It's designed to last for a good few hours. It shouldn't come off easily, but don't touch it to be on the safe side. Leave it alone when you go to bed—don't wash your face. You can take a bit with you,' she added, tipping the flesh-coloured liquid into a tiny plastic bottle. 'In case you need it—but it should still be pretty good in the morning if you're not a night-time dribbler.'

Matt laughed; he liked this high-energy woman.

'Your eye still looks a bit puffy,' said Elena. 'But you can just say a fly went into it or something, if anyone notices.'

'All good?' said Callie, snapping the make-up box shut. 'Because that pond won't dig itself.' She left the box on the table and ran back out into the garden, seizing the spade and singing out: 'HEIGH-HOOOOO!' like one of the seven dwarves.

Matt shook his head in wonder. 'She's amazing.'

'I know she is,' said Elena, glancing down at her hands. 'Crazy, but amazing.'

'You never let *me* say crazy,' pointed out Matt. 'Or mad or even bonkers.'

'That's right,' she said. 'You're not allowed. I am, though.'

'She seems great to me,' he said as he headed for the door.

'She is great,' agreed Elena. 'For now.'

'So . . .' he turned to her as he reached the front step. 'What's she like when she's not so great?'

'You don't want to know,' said Elena. He saw the shutters come down across her face and realized that he wasn't the only one who never grassed.

CHAPTER 7

'ZZZZZZZZZZZZZZZZZZZZZZZZZZ.
RRRRRRRRRRRRRRRRRR.
NINNNNNNNNNNNNNNNG.'

'Now you, Tima.'

'ZZZZZZZZZZZZZZZZZZZZZZZZZ.
RRRRRRRRRRRRRRRRRR.
NINNNNNNNNNNNNNNNG.'

'Now both of you.'

'ZZZZZZZZZZZZZZZZZZZZZZZZZZ.
RRRRRRRRRRRRRRRRRR.
NINNNNNNNNNNNNNNNG.'

'Excellent. Really good *N G* hum, Tima. Lily—work on yours—it's a bit nasal. It needs to be higher in your head cavity. Very nice *R* rolling, though. Nice, relaxed throat folds.'

Mr James beamed at his two soloists. 'This is going to be a great concert. I have a plan for you both.'

Lily swept back her blonde bob of hair, let out a tinkling laugh and said: 'Oh, Mr James! Don't keep us in suspense!'

'Well, I *was* thinking about giving you each a solo for the harvest festival concert,' he said, glancing from Tima to Lily. 'But the truth is there won't be enough space in the programme to give you *both* a solo.'

Tima stiffened. This did not sound good. If she got the solo, Lily and Lily's friends would make her school life hell. If Lily got the solo . . . well, then *Lily* would have got the solo. Her smugometer would break.

'So—I've decided you'll sing a duet.'

They gasped in perfect unison, as if they'd been practising.

A duet? With Lily Fry?! Tima felt her mouth drop open.

Lily recovered faster. In seconds she was pulling Tima into a hug, gushing: 'Oh, that will be *amazing*! I will *love* duetting with Tima!'

'Good,' said Mr James, flicking a slightly anxious glance at Tima. 'Because it's not an easy duet. You're really going to have to work hard together to pull it off.'

Tima gulped and then pasted a smile on her face. 'We can do it,' she said. 'What is it?'

'It's the "Flower Duet"—from the opera *Lakmé*, by Léo Delibes.'

Tima and Lily performed more synchronized gasping. 'An *opera*?' said Lily.

'Yes—an opera,' laughed Mr James. 'And I know that's

quite a leap from Nancy in *Oliver!*, but actually, I think you can both pull this off. We will simplify it and we won't be doing the whole piece, just the bit most people know, but I really think you can do it. Do you know the piece I mean? It was in that advert recently . . .'

They both nodded eagerly and Tima felt the weirdest mixture of excitement and freak-out. The 'Flower Duet' was wonderful—she had never imagined getting to perform it. But performing it with *Lily Fry*? Lily *loathed* her.

Tima didn't have much love for Lily either.

Lily and her friends, Clara and Kiera, had given Tima a hard time as soon as she'd arrived at Prince William Prep. It was never going to be easy starting at a school in Year Six— especially a school like PWP where best friends had been made back in pre-prep. After living in London for all of her life, Tima had been suddenly uprooted when her dad got a top job as a consultant surgeon at a private hospital in Suffolk. Her mum also got uprooted, of course, and was now establishing a new vet's practice. They were both from Yemen originally and although they'd lived in the UK for all of Tima's life, they still had a slight accent. Suffolk wasn't exactly teeming with Arabs, so they all occasionally had to deal with some 'awkwardness' from time to time. 'Awkwardness' was how Mum always put it.

Yeah.

Anyway, Lily and her friends had dished out a bit of minor 'awkwardness' as soon as Tima arrived in school. But it got a lot more awkward when the auditions for *Oliver!* were announced and Lily coolly declared to everyone that she was going to be

Nancy. Nobody argued. Lily was the school's most talented singer.

At least she *had* been, until Tima arrived.

When Tima got the role, despite the many audible mutterings that 'nobody ever heard of an *Arab* Nancy', Lily was in shock. She had stormed away from the noticeboard where the list of roles was posted, white with rage. Then she got a grip. By lunchtime that day Lily was telling everyone she had kindly stepped aside to allow the nervous little new girl to have a go. And she was *delighted* to take the lesser role of Nancy's friend, Bet. It was just the sort of thing you *should* do, to welcome foreigners.

After that it got pretty nasty whenever Lily and her friends got to chance to have a dig. Which was very often.

But that was all ancient history now. Lily was clearly *thrilled* about the 'Flower Duet'. *Thrilled.*

'We'll rehearse and rehearse,' she promised Mr James. 'Tima can come over to my house and we can rehearse there!'

Tima smiled weakly. 'We'll really work hard on it,' she said to Mr James, wishing Lily would let go of her arm.

'OK—here's the sheet music, the lyrics, and a CD for you to listen to,' said Mr James, handing them each a plastic wallet. 'Track one is an original recording of the duet being performed at the Royal Opera House in Covent Garden— but don't get nervous. You're not going to sing it the same way. I don't want you to sound like a pair of forty-year-old divas. I want you to sound like Year Seven girls. Track two is the backing track for you to get used to—just piano, although the school orchestra will be doing the actual concert. Oh—and the lyrics are in French. OK?' He grinned broadly and rubbed a hand through his curly brown hair. 'Nothing you can't handle, eh?'

Lily literally jumped up and down, finally releasing Tima's arm. 'NO! We'll be SO good!'

'You'll take the lower part, Lily,' he added. 'And Tima will take the higher part.'

Tima nodded, feeling her heart thump with excitement. Lily or no, this was a fantastic duet. Mum and Dad would be delighted; they loved a bit of opera.

'Good—have a listen and we'll begin rehearsals tomorrow,' said Mr James.

They wandered, dazed, out of the music block.

'Wow,' said Tima, as they emerged on to the edge of the school's beautiful, tree-dotted grounds. 'I wasn't expecting that.'

'Me neither,' said Lily, eyeing her warily. 'I hope you can manage the French language.'

'I hope *you* can,' retorted Tima, raising an eyebrow.

'Oh, I'm fluent,' said Lily, breezily. 'Mummy and Daddy have a chateau in the Dordogne. We go for weeks every summer and Mummy says I talk like a native.'

'Well, good for you,' muttered Tima. *She* went for holidays with her family back in Yemen and could speak a bit of Arabic but she didn't say it. There was no point in competing with Lily.

'Au revoir,' said Lily and skipped away to find her friends.

Tima sat down on a lichen-painted brick wall, set the plastic wallet down at her feet, and marvelled at the weirdness of life.

She couldn't wait to tell Elena and Matt about *this*. Now she would really have to try to get on with Lily.

Zzzzzzzzzzzzzzzzzzzzzzzzzzzzzzzz.

Goosebumps suddenly ran across Tima's arms and shoulders. She glanced down at the brick wall. *Someone needs me.* She saw three bees. Two were circling around a third, which was resting, face down, on a ridge of moss. The resting bee—a female buff-tailed bumble, she was pretty sure—was not in a good way.

'Oh no, what's up?' she murmured, getting off the wall to turn and kneel against it, her chin resting right by the bees.

The two lively bumbles continued to circle the weak one. She could see it was drooping, its feelers limp. Its fur was coated in bright orange pollen and the tiny pouches on its back legs were full of it. Maybe it had overloaded itself.

Shall I get her a drink? she asked the others. *Some sugar water?* She reached into the pocket of her pinafore dress to find the tiny plastic bottle of sugar water she kept there out of habit these days. She'd saved a few bees from exhaustion this way. But the circling bees did not seem to think this would help. What they were sending her was . . . worrying. They were . . .

'Are you *scared*?' she murmured, softly. Both bees paused in their circling and faced her, feelers working agitatedly. 'What's happened?'

The bees went back to circling. They did not touch their fallen friend but she noticed they were fanning their wings, as if to keep it cool. Tima went to unscrew her sugar-water bottle anyway but suddenly the two companion bees stopped circling and fanning. For a few seconds they froze and then they abruptly flew away. Too late. The poorly bee was dead. Tima sighed and put the sugar-water bottle back in her pocket. She sent a little *I'm sorry I couldn't help* message to the departed insect and turned to pick up her sheet music and CD wallet.

She turned back, thinking she might collect the bee's tiny body and deposit it under some nearby rose bushes. And then she froze. The bee's body was not the same. It had turned dark brown—as if it had been burnt. How had *that* happened? Some kind of spontaneous combustion? She glanced up and around. It was a warm, sunny day but not *that* hot.

She stared back at the brown remains and then let out a yelp of shock. The remains were now no more than dust. A light breeze blew through her hair and fanned the dust out into a mist. And then there was nothing left.

Tima stepped away from the wall, clutching the plastic wallet to her chest. The bees had been scared.

So was she.

CHAPTER 8

Fur always made things better.

Elena felt her breathing slow and her hot, puffy face cool as she sat on the edge of the patio in the back garden. The fox sitting next to her didn't say anything. It didn't nuzzle her face or place a comforting paw on her knee. It just leant against her, ever so slightly, and looked up at the night sky.

Sometimes Elena thought Velma knew everything that was going on in her head. The vixen had been dropping in to see her for some months now. Not every night, just once or twice a week. Sometimes it would quietly slip out of the woods or undergrowth while she was walking to meet Tima or Matt. They would walk together for a while, content in each other's company. Occasionally Elena would bring along a treat for Velma—a bit of chicken or bacon or something—but Velma did not expect it. This wasn't about food. They had shared stuff. They had a friendship.

Tonight she had told Velma things. She hadn't spoken out loud, but she could have if she'd wanted to. Above her, Mum's bedroom window was dark and slightly open. Mum wouldn't have heard her speak, though. Elena had seen to it that she'd taken all her meds after dinner and she was deeply asleep. Thank God.

I know she can't help it, Elena sent to Velma. *She's ill.*

Velma yawned, her tongue curling delicately past her sharp fangs before her jaws snapped closed again.

Elena sighed. It had not been a good evening. Why on earth had she got Mum started on making the pond? It had seemed like a good idea at the time. Mum's mania was still breaking through the medication and Elena needed to direct all that energy into something intense and physical—but harmless— until it settled down. Digging. A pond. It had been working well when Matt had come over after school yesterday, but of course, Mum hadn't been able to stop at just digging.

When Elena had got home that day the front room was full of stuff. Mum had gone out in the car to buy underlay and a liner for the pond. But she hadn't stopped there. She'd got a pump, a filter, a small fountain kit for the centre, solar-powered lighting, aquatic plants, a wooden escape ramp for distressed hedgehogs, three books on aquatic gardening, and a whole sink-full of aquatic plants in sealed plastic bags of water.

The purchases were scattered across the carpet and sofa and her mother was at the laptop, finger poised over BUY NOW on a tank full of koi carp for sale on Amazon at an eye-watering sum. Elena had run, tripping over the small fountain kit, and swiped her mother's hands away from the keyboard just in time.

'What are you DOING?' Mum shrieked.

'What am *I* doing?' shrieked back Elena. 'What is all *this*? MUM! I thought we agreed! We said NO MORE SPENDING! NO MORE!'

And instead of arguing Mum did something worse. She stared around as if she was seeing it all for the first time, then she put her hands to her mouth and began to shake. She was crying all the while Elena was on the phone to Thornleigh WaterWorld, begging the manager to let her bring everything back and refund Mum's credit card. She cried as Elena grimly packed everything into the boot of a taxi and got it back to the shop which, thank God, was still open and—thank God even *more*—had a decent human being for a manager, who had heard of bipolar disorder. He seemed to understand as he ran all the goods back through the till in reverse and gave Elena a receipt to prove the refund on Mum's card. He didn't even ask to see her Young Carer ID.

Mum was still crying, a little, when Elena got home. She stopped when Elena sat her down and made her eat sausages, chips, and beans, followed by her pills and some orange squash. 'I'm so sorry,' she kept saying. 'I'm so rubbish. You should've had a good mum. I'm so sorry.' Elena took all the credit and debit cards and hid them in her bedroom. She shuddered to think of all the things Mum might have bought that she *didn't* know about. She would find out when the bills came through next month. They would probably be living on budget baked beans and super-saver bread until Christmas. She should have said no to getting the broadband connection back . . . but that was in the summer when Mum had seemed so well. Maybe she should get it disconnected again.

Mum had fallen into bed just after nine. And now it was time to sit in the garden and have a bit of a cry herself. With Velma to lean on. Where was this going to end? She should call Dr Cohen. She *should*. But then what? What would Dr Cohen do once he knew the mania still hadn't subsided? Elena shivered. She hadn't forgotten what had happened two years ago, and she'd do almost *anything* to stop that happening again.

'Velma,' she said, aloud. 'Do you give your cubs this much trouble?'

Velma leant harder against her and flicked a fine pointed ear against her neck.

It was nearly ten o'clock and she should be getting to bed. The few short hours between bedtime and 1.34 a.m. were her best sleep hours. Most nights she tried to get to bed by 9.30 p.m., just as soon as she'd settled Mum. If she was lucky she might get three hours before the beam came through—and then, after her night-time wanderings with Tima and Matt, she might get another hour or two around dawn. Last night they hadn't met up at all; Tima was out late at some party with her parents and Matt had decided to just stay home and play video games all night. So Elena had awoken at 1.34 a.m. and picked up a book, which kept her occupied until sleep finally reclaimed her around five. She was looking forward to catching up with Matt and

Tima tonight—to getting out of the house where her drugged mother lay in dreamless sleep.

Elena leant her cheek on Velma's furry head and closed her eyes for a moment. She felt the vixen suddenly stiffen and snapped her eyes open again. A dark shadow loomed in front of her.

'Sweet,' it said, as Velma fled into the hedge.

Elena got up, tension flooding back into her. 'Spin. What are you doing here?'

'Well, *that's* a nice greeting for a friend,' he said, sitting down on the edge of the patio with a waft of his black silk coat. Elena could sense Velma watching from the hedge, ready to defend her if necessary.

'Friends don't loom up out of the dark uninvited,' she said, eyeing him coldly. 'And on that point—please remember—I *didn't* invite you.' Her hand went instinctively to the chain around her throat.

He laughed. 'I love that you know the rules,' he said. 'But back gardens are open to me. I don't need an invitation. Your *house* is different. But we're not in your house, are we?' He tilted his pale face and narrowed his blue-green eyes.

Clutching the pendant on the chain, she lifted her chin. And then tucked it down again, hurriedly.

'Oh my! What have we got *here?*' Suddenly he was on his feet, face full of merriment, reaching for her pendant. She slapped his hand away, feeling furious heat rise through her cheeks. 'No really—you have to let me see!' he said, gurgling with laughter. 'Is it . . . could it be . . . a little *crucifix?*'

'Just shut up and go away,' she snapped. 'I'm not in the mood for your stupid games.'

His grin slid a little as he looked at her more closely. 'No. You're not, are you?' He touched her face before she could stop him and then pulled back his hand, rubbing his fingertips together. 'Tears? What's gone wrong, Mona Lisa?'

She scrubbed at her cheeks, annoyed at his stupid nickname for her. She was no oil painting right now. 'What's wrong? Other than *you* showing up? Nothing.'

'Aah, but it's not nothing, is it?' His eyes roamed the garden, lit by the square of gold that spilt from the kitchen window, and then travelled up to the dark bedroom window above. 'Trouble at home?'

For a second she teetered on the brink of telling him. Then she pressed her lips together. No. She could not trust Spin. He was too unpredictable. He had been a kind of ally back in the early summer when they'd all fought the underworld god . . . but probably only because he was in danger too. Since then she'd seen nothing of him—although she'd sensed him stalking them all several times. Spin liked to stalk and listen in.

'Why are you here?' she asked.

'Wanted to check you're not *too* bruised from our last encounter,' he said, looking back towards her.

She touched her forehead. She'd borrowed Mum's make-up and easily covered the bruise but it was still tender. 'What was *that* about?'

He frowned, looking quite uncharacteristically serious for a moment. 'I was kind of hoping you might be able to tell *me*.'

She shrugged. 'All *I* know was that me and Tima found you lying in the grass like a corpse. And when we tried to help you, you headbutted me and scratched Tima's face.'

'Ouch! Did I? That doesn't sound like me at *all*,' he said. No word of apology.

'Well, it *was* you. We really thought you were . . . dead.'

'What—with no stake through my heart?' he said, arching an eyebrow. She folded her arms and shook her head. 'OK—I'll tell you what happened,' he said, abruptly sitting back down on the edge of the patio. 'I was out . . . er . . . *entertaining* the good people of Thornleigh.'

'Stalking?' She sat too, but at a distance.

'No. *Attacking*. But I didn't get very far. My prey got lucky. Someone interrupted my fun; a woman. Youngish—about twenty, I'd say. Long dark hair, leather outfit, nice boots . . . She wanted directions.'

'In the middle of the night?' Elena found herself intrigued. 'Directions to where?'

'To nurseries,' he said. He ran black-varnished nails through his white-blond hair. 'That's what she wanted; a list of nurseries in the Thornleigh area.'

'OK,' said Elena. 'That *is* bit odd. Did she say why?'

'No . . . I imagine she wanted to collect babies for experimenting on,' he said.

'You *would* think that,' she said. 'Maybe she meant a plants nursery. You know, like a garden centre?'

'Hmmm. Good point. Either way, I couldn't help,' he said.

'And then what?'

'Well, I was . . . *not helping* . . .'

'Oh right. You decided to freak her out,' cottoned on Elena.

'You know me so well.'

'I know you just as much as I want to,' she said. 'And that's enough. So—what happened?'

'She shot me in the face.'

Elena blinked. 'Really?'

'Oh yes. *Bang! You're dead.* Not a bullet, though, as it turns out. After I'd done my Sleeping Beauty awakening—and my Cinderella fleeing—'

'Back to your Shrek swamp?'

'Nice one. Yes. After I'd got back to the swamp I discovered she'd blasted me with some kind of sticky knock-out juice. No lasting damage.' He smiled, nodding. 'She has style.'

'So—no ill effects at all?' Elena asked. He'd looked *so* dead that was hard to believe.

'Not so far as I know,' he said. He got to his feet. 'Anyway, you clearly can't offer any more information. The night is young. Stuff to do.'

She stood too. 'Nothing else to say to me?'

'Aaah . . .' He frowned and looked sideways. 'Nope.'

'No *"Sorry for headbutting you?"*.'

'Never apologize. Never explain,' he said. Then he vanished in a puff of smoke.

An *actual* puff of smoke.

CHAPTER 9

'We need a den,' said Matt.

'A den?' echoed Tima. 'Oooh—that's so *Famous Five!*'

Matt winced. 'I'm not talking about a cosy little hut with your mum bringing us scones and tea,' he muttered, stroking Lucky's dark, feathered head. 'But it's autumn now and soon it'll be winter and too cold to be out in the middle of the night. That's if we're going to carry on doing this . . .' He paused. 'Of course, the beam might stop at any time and we might start being normal and sleeping again.'

Tima and Elena exchanged glances as they lounged on the wooden deck of the bandstand. Neither of them looked keen on this possibility, which pleased Matt more than he'd ever admit. 'Anyway—assuming that doesn't happen and we go on being these insomnia freaks—we need somewhere warm to meet up to pass the time.'

'What have you got in mind?' asked Elena.

Matt grinned. 'I found a place.'

'Where?' demanded Tima.

'Well, actually, it was Lucky who found it,' he added.

Lucky paused in preening a wing to comment: 'Lucky.' Matt could never be sure whether she was just parroting him when she spoke or *really* making a comment. Starlings were brilliant mimics—he'd found this out in bird books from the library—but could she really be *talking* to them? Now he was a Night Speaker, it was difficult to tell, because he and any kind of bird connected these days. None quite as much as Lucky, though. And yes—it *was* lucky. Together they'd found something brilliant.

'Come *on*,' said Tima. 'Don't keep us in suspense—what have you found?'

'It's on the other side of Leigh Hill,' he said. 'About ten minutes' walk from here. Come on. I'll show you.'

He *did* keep them in suspense, the whole way. He couldn't resist it. He sent Lucky home to sleep, because she wasn't a nocturnal animal and he didn't like to keep her up too often overnight. A bird's energy, he knew from his reading, was a finely balanced thing. They took a cut through a small copse behind a housing estate, following a dark, winding stream, and then ducked under the looming brick arch of a railway viaduct and climbed a steep incline to the south-western end of the town. Then it was down a slope into a densely wooded area far from any ramblers' paths.

'How did you find this place . . . whatever it is?' puffed Elena, sliding a little on some loose, gravelly scree as they plunged further into the dark trees, her torch beam dancing ahead of her.

'I didn't. Like I said, Lucky did. I just told her we needed somewhere dry and warm to meet up when the winter came. Asked her if she knew of any place where no other people went. She took me there after school today.' Matt grabbed a tree branch to stop himself sliding down the steep hillside.

'Oh—how was school?' asked Tima. 'Any more trouble with your bullies?'

'They're *not* my bullies,' snapped Matt. 'Nobody bullies *me*.'

'OK—not your bullies. Those nice boys who kicked your head in,' amended Tima, ducking under a low sprig of holly.

'They're all suspended,' said Matt. 'So it was a quiet day. But I had to go and work in the school garden all lunchtime with weird Mr Janssen—make up for the broken netting and the smashed up melons and marrows.'

'How is he weird?' asked Elena. 'I've seen him. He's very tall but he seems normal enough.'

'I don't know,' said Matt. 'He doesn't say much. He stands around staring into space a lot. He made me dig a new vegetable patch. It was OK, though. I didn't mind.' In truth, he couldn't pin down exactly why Mr Janssen seemed weird. There was something very intense about him and his eyes were a peculiarly pale shade of blue; like the inside of an iceberg. When Matt had tried to follow him into his greenhouse to return the spade and fork at the end of his working lunch hour, Janssen had turned

52

to him and said, very slowly and deliberately: *'You do not come in here.'*

He couldn't blame the guy. He thought Matt was a troublemaker. A thug. A 'crim' as Elena and Tima often delighted in calling him. Loads of people thought that about him; apparently it was his face. He just *looked* criminal.

'We're here,' he said and stopped at the foot of a clump of trees.

Elena and Tima looked around, sending their torch beams flickering across trunks and branches. They looked at him blankly. 'So . . . we're just going to hide in the woods when it snows?' said Elena. 'That's your plan?'

He grinned again and shone his own torch beam slowly upwards. Gratifyingly they both went 'Oooooooh!' A closer look at the clump of trees revealed something unexpected. Five young oaks had grown close together, tall and strong, reaching up amid a thicket of holly bushes. A person could step in between the trunks and only then would they notice something unusual. A thin metal ladder, choked with ivy, rose between the trees, anchored into their roots. It offered a five-metre climb into the leafy canopy, disappearing into a square black hole in the underside of a wooden platform.

'A tree house!' squeaked Tima.

'A hide,' corrected Matt. 'Forestry Commission put it up years ago.' He tucked his slim torch, base down, into the pocket of his thick checked shirt, where it threw the light upwards, and began to climb the metal rungs. He reached the hole in the wooden platform and hauled himself up through it, kneeling on the dry, leaf-choked floor, and leant down to help Tima up.

She and Elena scrambled up into the hide and shone their torches around, looking thrilled. It was the size of a large shed, sturdily built across the branches of the oaks. It was roughly rectangular but two of its corners were accommodating the stout posts of ever-growing tree trunks. The roof was pitched at an angle and on one side there was a long, narrow, letterbox-style open window with a broad wooden sill. Perfect for bird watchers.

'This is brilliant!' said Elena. 'But won't we get into trouble if we just help ourselves to it? Isn't it *owned* by the Forestry Commission?'

Matt threw his light up to the roof. There were a couple of planks missing from it. Leafy branches reached through it and cascades of dead leaves drifted below the gap. 'This hasn't been visited in ages,' he said. 'Lucky says nobody's been here all of her life. I don't think anyone's bothering with it these days.'

'Hmmm,' said Tima, peering up. 'It's not going to be too dry in the winter, is it? Or warm.'

Matt scowled. 'I didn't order it from *Dens R Us*! I'm not saying it's perfect. We need to mend the roof—clear out the dead leaves and stuff. Maybe put some thick plastic across the windows for when it gets colder.'

'We could bring stuff to sit on; boxes, blankets, and cushions,' said Elena, starting to grin. 'Maybe even a little paraffin stove to keep warm and make tea. I think we've got a camping stove in the shed.'

Tima turned, nodding, like a prospective house buyer. 'OK—it needs work—but I think it'll do.'

'Well, don't do me any favours,' said Matt, huffing a little.

'It's brilliant!' said Tima, launching herself at him with a theatrical hug. 'You're so clever to think of it!'

'All right, all right.' Matt disengaged himself awkwardly; he'd never get used to Tima's hugs. 'Don't overdo it.'

Elena was surveying the ceiling in her torchlight. 'We're not the only ones living here,' she said, smiling. A moment later there was a drumming of tiny feet on the other side of the planks and two small furry faces pushed through the invading twigs and leaves and peered down at them. 'Hello,' said Elena.

'Aaaaw! They're so *cute*!' Tima beamed up at the squirrels. 'Will they mind if we move in?'

Elena shook her head, reaching a hand up towards the squirrels. 'Careful,' said Matt. 'They can really bite.'

'As *if*,' said Elena. She rested her hand on a sturdy twig, close to the two small mammals, and one of them elegantly leapt on to her forearm, clinging to her fleecy sleeve and balancing with its bushy grey tail. Elena carefully lowered her arm, holding it out like a steady branch, and stared delightedly into the dark round eyes of the squirrel. 'They live in a drey just a short climb up above the roof,' she said. 'They've got four babies. They want to know they'll be safe.' She tentatively put out a finger and stroked the squirrel's head, just between its perky ears. It didn't bite her. She didn't speak for a few seconds; just lowered her head until she and the small mammal were literally nose to nose.

The squirrel stayed perfectly still, its tail wrapped tightly around her wrist, and Matt found himself breaking out in goosebumps as he watched the unspoken communication between human and animal. It was just the same between him and birds, and he knew, if he worked a little harder, that he could probably reach squirrels and foxes and other mammals like Elena could. Even speak to insects, like Tima. But each of them seemed to have a different Night Speaking affinity and it felt comfortable to stay with their chosen group of animals. Together they seemed to have it all covered.

Elena lifted her head, and then her arm, and the squirrel ran up on to her fist, paused to look back down at her, and then leapt up to join its mate who had been watching overhead. A few scrambles and they were gone.

'I've told them we'll be extra careful while we mend the roof,' she said. 'And said we might bring a few nuts for their babies.'

'Oooh! I want to feed peanuts to baby squirrels!' squeaked Tima, leaping lightly up and down.

'Well, maybe,' said Elena. 'We'll let them get used to us first. I asked her to pass on the word that we're not here to harm anything else in the trees. I think we're all good.'

'So then,' said Matt. 'Either of you any good with a hammer and nails?'

Tima gave a hollow laugh. 'Me? Seriously?'

'I can hammer in a nail,' said Elena. 'I've put up shelves and stuff at home.'

'I'll be good for decoration,' offered Tima, resting both elbows back on the deep wooden sill of the hide window and scanning the room. 'I've got loads of little LED lights and stuff. Oh—someone wants you.' She moved away from the windowsill and Matt saw a plump bundle of brown feathers perched on it. The tawny owl gave him a hard stare from its orb-shaped dark eyes and made a small *ke-wick* noise. Matt let out a sharp, low curse.

'What's up?' asked Elena, glancing between Matt and the owl.

'Message from Lucky,' said Matt, grimacing. 'Dad's up. Moving about the flat. Hasn't checked in on my room yet but he could do at any time. I have to go.'

'Go then,' said Elena. 'We'll make our own way back.'

Matt felt uneasy but before he could say anything Elena insisted: '*Go!* We'll be perfectly safe without you. Remember we can call on an army of stinging insects or a platoon of killer squirrels any time we need to!' She was only half joking. 'The biggest danger right now,' she added, seriously, 'is to you. Get home and get into bed before he finds out.'

Matt lost no more time arguing.

CHAPTER 10

Tima and Elena made their way back through the woods and along the quiet, dark roads of Thornleigh, talking in low voices, instinctively dodging very occasional passing drivers by sliding into the trees or behind bus shelters and tall vans. This had become second nature to them now as they roamed the town by night.

Sometimes they noticed the movement of headlights and slipped away into shadow but more often they were warned well before the lights were visible. Usually Tima got the vibe first, as her insect friends were flying and able to see further than many of Elena's mammal buddies. The warnings would be hard to describe to anyone who wasn't a Night Speaker; they were something like a change in vibration, a twitch in pitch of the night noise, a thickening of the atmospheric pressure, or an almost imperceptible shift of scent, drifting in the air. So fine and subtle that you had to be tuned in to know; sometimes it was little more than a prickling of the fine hairs on their forearms. Warnings. Guidance. Help.

'I saw Spin earlier,' said Elena, as they stepped back out from a bus shelter and walked on, the motorist safely gone.

'Why didn't you say?' demanded Tima. 'Where was he? What was he doing?!'

'He came round my place,' said Elena.

'What?!' Tima spun around and grabbed her arms. 'You *never* invited him in!'

'Of *course* not,' said Elena. 'He just showed up in my back garden. I was sitting out there with Velma for a while and he did his lurk-y thing. Out of nowhere. You know what he's like.'

Tima *did* know what Spin was like. The first time she'd ever seen him he'd been floating among the trees like a shroud of death—then he'd chased her in the form of smoke, laughing maniacally. She'd been absolutely certain she was about to die. Happily Elena and Matt had come to her rescue; that was how she'd met them, so at least she had *something* to thank Spin for.

'Well? What did he want?' she asked.

'I did think for one crazy moment that he'd come to apologize for headbutting me and scratching your face—but no chance of that. Saying sorry isn't really his style, is it?'

'So . . . he wasn't after a nice neckful of your blood?' Tima narrowed her eyes.

'No,' said Elena. She pulled the little cross out on its chain. 'I had this on, just in case.'

'So then—what? He hasn't shown up in weeks and now he's back. Playing dead one minute; creeping around your garden the next. What does he want?'

'He told me he'd been shot in the face with some kind of, I dunno, chemical taser? That's why we found him lying under the hedge, looking like a corpse. He said this woman did it—some woman dressed in leather. She was looking for something . . . a nursery. Anyway, sounds like he wound her up with his vampire act, so she shot him.'

'Bravo, her!' said Tima, clapping her hands and falling back into step beside Elena as they neared her road. 'Hey, wait . . . she was dressed in *leather*?'

'Yeah. Leather gear and nice boots, or so Spin said.' Elena shrugged. 'He's in touch with fashion, apparently.'

'Hmmm, shall we *not* take him shopping, though?' said Tima. 'Um . . . this woman. *I* met a woman wearing leather the night before last. She was looking for something she'd dropped in the grass just across the street. Over there.' She pointed to the grassy verge opposite her house, which had just come into view. 'She was asking about nurseries too. Sounds like the same one!'

'Maybe,' said Elena.

'Well anyway—be careful,' said Tima, dropping her voice even lower as they reached the high, brick pillars on either side of the driveway to her home. 'I know he kind of helped us out back in the summer but he can't be trusted. He's probably stalking us again.' She glanced around suspiciously. 'Listening in. Don't encourage him.'

'I *don't* encourage him!' hissed Elena. 'Tee, you're as bad as

Matt! I didn't mention it before because I knew he'd really kick off about it. He *hates* Spin.'

'Yeah, he does. Spin's the only other boy who's been able to beat him up, one-on-one, that's why,' said Tima. 'All that kung fu stuff. Do you think he really *is* a vampire?'

Elena laughed. 'Of course not.' But Tima could see she wasn't sure. 'He can't be,' Elena said, rolling her eyes, 'but he has got some good special effects going on. All that black smoke and disappearing and floating about in trees.'

'Just keep your cross on,' said Tima. 'Since May, I believe in *everything*. I mean, if we can talk to animals and there are underworld gods beneath Thornleigh, a real-life vampire is *nothing*. See you tomorrow. Usual time and place. I'll bring my LED fairy lights.'

She headed inside and up to bed. Dawn was close but she thought she'd probably get a couple of hours of sleep in. Up the stairs, sleek as a cat and almost as noiseless, she stopped on the landing. Gah! She'd completely forgotten to tell Elena about the dead bee. All the tree house excitement and then the Spin stuff had pushed it out of her mind. She'd have to talk to them both about it tomorrow.

In her room she threw off her burglar gear and went for one last glance out between her curtains. Then she saw something was stuck to the window. A red circle, about the size of a coin, firmly attached to the other side of the glass.

She unlatched the window, peering around it to stare at the thing which clung to it. *'What?'* she murmured to herself. The red circle was the sucker end of a toy arrow. Someone had shot

61

a *toy arrow* at her window! The little red rubber disc was firmly suctioned on, its yellow shaft pointing out at a firm ninety-degree angle. And the stick part was wrapped tightly in paper. The arrow came away from the glass with a small pop and she brought it back into her room to examine it by lamplight. Her first thought—that some kid had just been messing around and couldn't get their toy arrow back—evaporated as she unrolled the paper. It was long and thin and filled with tiny, spidery handwriting. A message. For her. It read:

Hello. You helped me search for my inhaler. Thank you. I need your help again. Can you meet me at midnight? I will be waiting in the same place. Just you, please. It's important. Carra

Tima stared at the message. It must have arrived after she'd left in the early hours; there had been nothing on her window when she'd got up at 1.34am. How bizarre.

Just you, please. It's important.

Really? Elena might be the 'sensible one' in their little club, but Tima wasn't an idiot. Helping out when she was passing was one thing, but she wasn't going out to meet a virtual stranger in the dead of night, on her own.

But . . . after what Elena had told her, she *was* intrigued. Was this the same woman who'd shot Spin in the face? If nothing else, Tima quite fancied shaking her by the hand for that. It wasn't that she *wanted* Spin to be shot in the face, not really. Not even with some kind of chemical spray that only made him conk out . . . it was just that he so often had the upper hand and was so superior. And menacing. He'd never apologized to her about all that sinister chasing business back in the summer either. Whatever the leather-clad woman had done to him, frankly, he'd had it coming.

Tima got into bed. She would decide after some sleep. Maybe she'd meet her; maybe not. *Oh, of course you're going to meet her!* chided an inner voice. *Shut up*, she replied. *I'm going to sleep now.*

CHAPTER 11

'The bright green ones. Those. Take those out.'

Matt squinted up at Mr Janssen as he towered above him, blotting out the sun. 'What—*all* of them?'

'Yes. All of them,' said the groundsman. He pronounced 'of' as 'off'. He was not friendly. He certainly wasn't making any effort to get Matt interested in gardening, heading back into his steamy plastic greenhouse at every opportunity with only the occasional cough to remind Matt he was even there.

Matt sighed and turned back to the weeds. They were bright green, with tiny rounded leaves, and they were *everywhere*, running like green lace around the base of all the cauliflowers and cabbages. They weren't deeply rooted but Mr Janssen had told him he must pull carefully and shake them free of the soil, or risk leaving the roots in to continue their invasion.

There was nothing else for it. He was in for another dull lunch break, pulling up weeds and chucking them in a bucket. He'd stuffed his sandwiches on the way down across the field and now had half an hour of gardening fun. Still, he knew he should be grateful. It could have been so much worse. Two days after the fight, his bruises were fading to yellow and the scratch was healing well. Each morning, after washing, he'd applied a little of the magical paint that Elena's mum had made for him, and so far Dad hadn't noticed his wounds.

This didn't mean everything was fine. Life at home wasn't ever fine. Not really. Since his older brother Ben had left to join the navy, Matt had been taking the brunt of the shoves and slaps and occasional full-on beatings from Dad, usually after his father had drunk half a bottle of brandy. Since his time in the hospital in the early summer, Matt had noticed Dad restraining himself a bit. But the odd angry cuff or shove was creeping back into their everyday exchanges—when Matt forgot to switch the vacuum off and wasted the electricity for two minutes; when he dropped a bottle of wax on to a windscreen and could have cracked it (but hadn't); when he missed a wheel arch because he was too busy staring at birds (Lucky had been waiting for him to finish and go for a walk with her).

Most of the time it was no big deal. He was used to Dad and didn't think the man would ever *seriously* hurt him. He wasn't a psychopath, just a short-tempered bruiser. And sometimes he was OK. When things were going well—if his team had just won a match or he'd got a generous tip from a regular customer—he could be nice. It was just that Matt

6 5

couldn't trust him to stay that way. Dad was like a cranky old bulldog—sometimes lovable but always ready to bite.

'You haf finished.'

Matt jumped, wincing as little stabs of pain went through his battered ribs, and looked up to see Mr Janssen standing behind him again. He got up, chucking the last few weeds into the bucket. He'd cleared the patch completely, as far as he could tell.

'You work fast,' said Mr Janssen.

'I'm used to it,' said Matt, with a shrug. 'Working fast, I mean—not gardening. I work fast cleaning cars.'

'You haf no need to return,' said Mr Janssen. 'Your debt is paid.' He pulled his face into something resembling a smile.

Matt brushed the soil off his hands. 'OK . . . er . . . thanks.'

He headed back into school, went into the boys' toilets to wash the grime out from under his fingernails, and then headed for the library for the last ten minutes of lunch break. As he walked along the corridor it was a relief to know he wasn't going to bump into Liam or Ahmed or any of the others. He'd never really thought about how wound up they made him feel but he now realized that for the first time in weeks, months . . . maybe even *years* . . . he wasn't wandering around school with his belly in a hard knot.

He passed the head teacher's office and paused. Mr Rosen's door was open. He was spraying something on one of his plants—a rather weird-looking orchid-like thing with white blooms and orange-tipped green leaves. Mr Rosen suddenly looked up and smiled and waved Matt in. 'I hear you've done good work down in the kitchen garden,' he said, as Matt approached.

Matt shrugged. 'Mr Janssen said I was all done, though. Debt paid. I don't think he wants me hanging around, really.'

'That sounds like him,' said Mr Rosen. 'Likes to keep himself to himself.' He stroked the orange-tipped leaves of the orchid. 'Thought he was just your standard groundskeeper when I took him on but he's passionate about plants. I think he's planning to get some hybrids into some local shows. It's fine by me as long as he keeps growing such good stuff for the school kitchen. And beauties like this!'

'They're . . . nice,' said Matt, lamely. Plants weren't really his thing.

'Anyway,' said Mr Rosen, sitting back down behind his desk, puffing slightly. 'Well done for making amends. Now you can get back to the library in your lunch breaks.'

Matt blinked, surprised, and the head teacher laughed, mopping his slightly sweaty brow with a hanky. 'Oh, not much gets past me, you know. Mrs Jeffers says you're a librarian's dream—the boy who came in from the cold! She loves it when she converts anyone to the printed page.'

Matt smiled. Mrs Jeffers would willingly have locked the library door on him six months ago. He'd been about as welcome in a library as a fox in a henhouse. He and his former mates used to go in from time to time, loudly eat crisps, and annoy the swots. But once she'd realized he really *did* want to find out stuff from books, Mrs Jeffers melted into his best book buddy. She'd even tried to get him signed up to the local Young Bird

6 7

Watchers Club. She'd failed on that. He wasn't planning to stand around in an anorak, noting lesser spotted bearded warblers in the local marshes all weekend. Truth was, he didn't need to. If there *was* such a thing as a lesser spotted bearded warbler in the area, Lucky would find it for him and make the introductions.

'Thanks again, sir,' he said, turning to go. 'Oh—sorry—you've got a dead one.' He pointed to the tropical fish tank where a pale blue fish was floating jerkily on the surface, buffeted by bubbles from the oxygenator.

'Oh dear,' said Mr Rosen, getting up to see. 'That's the second tetra I've lost this week. Ah well.'

Matt left him to his deceased fish and headed to the library. He was hoping to find a DIY book which covered the building and mending of tree houses. He couldn't wait to get started on their hide.

CHAPTER 12

'I know I shouldn't ask,' said Mrs Patel. 'But is she doing OK?'

Elena smiled tightly.

'Ah,' said Mrs Patel, nodding. She pushed the packet of medication across the counter and glanced around the small pharmacy. It was empty, so she clearly felt emboldened to go on. 'It's none of my business, but I think you are doing a marvellous job. If you ever need any help or advice, do come and find me. Bipolar is a really hard thing to manage for anyone, let alone a young thing like you.'

'We manage fine,' said Elena, feeling both defensive and touched. She had been collecting Mum's medication from Patel's for three years now. She remembered the first time, holding out her Young Carer card with a shaking hand; proof that the NHS had decided she was responsible enough to be given high-octane drugs to take home to her mother. Mrs Patel, to her credit, hadn't questioned her. She hadn't even raised her eyebrows. She'd just read the prescription, nodded, smiled warmly at her, and then gone to the dispensary, returning with paper packets full of the stuff that would make her mother normal again. Maybe.

Today the pharmacist was just as sensitive. She understood Elena's reaction. She smiled that warm smile once again and nodded. 'You manage very well,' she said. 'But the offer is still there. Wait a moment,' she double-checked the packets. 'I need to give you ten more lithium.' She wandered back through the dispensary as her son Mohammed came in from the storeroom behind, carrying bottles and packets.

'We need more Ventolin,' he said, sitting at a bench at the back and sorting through his supplies.

'More?'

'Yep. And Clenil. It's inhaler central here this week. Everybody wants some.' After a pause, he added: 'Is she OK?'

'She's OK,' sighed Mrs Patel. 'Well, as OK as any fourteen-year-old can be when her mum's got bipolar disorder and her waste-of-space father skipped out without a backward glance.'

Elena froze, feeling her face suddenly heat up. *What?!*

'These kids deserve a medal,' went on Mrs Patel, at normal volume, just as if she wasn't there. 'I mean, it's not Callie's fault—she's a lovely woman—but when she gets manic or depressed, it's her daughter who has to be the mum. I get really angry when I think about the father, just leaving her to it. What kind of man would do that? She's a teenager. She should be having fun.'

Elena felt her mouth fall open. She had never heard anyone

say this out loud. Ever. She'd suspected some people *thought* it, but never, ever expected to hear them say it.

'She'll be OK,' went on Mohammed, still sorting through his boxes. 'She's really together for a kid. Pretty, too.'

'Enough of that,' chided Mrs Patel. She glanced across at Elena as if to verify her prettiness, and then clocked the expression on her young customer's face. Mrs Patel blinked. She glanced back at Mohammed and then back at Elena, looking both baffled and mortified.

'Are you OK, sweetheart?' she said, coming to the counter, tugging nervously at her pale blue headscarf. She put the pills down.

Elena snatched them up and ran out, shaking with shock and humiliation. How *dare* they talk about her mum and her dad like that, right in front of her? She heard Mrs Patel call after her but she didn't look back, she just broke into a run, stuffing the meds into her school bag.

When she reached the park area near her home she ran across the grass and found a quiet bench under the trees. She sank on to it, snatching deep lungfuls of air, trying to get her pulse to go back to normal. Since becoming a Night Speaker she had dealt with unimaginable freakery. But Mrs Patel's casual conversation in her earshot had freaked her out on a whole new level. Not just because of what she'd said—there was nothing much in *that* to shock Elena and, frankly, the pharmacist had a point. It was the *way* she'd said it. Talking so personally about a customer, right in front of them, broke every taboo going. What was going on? Was Mrs Patel going madder than Mum?

She only realized she was crying when her tears were licked off by a small mammal. She'd been vaguely aware that she had company; tiny paws padding across her lap and arm and shoulder, soft fur tickling at her skin. She had two visitors. The one on her lap stretched its grey paws up on to her chest and looked her right in the eyes while the other nestled into her hair and took a warm lick of salty tears off her cheek. Elena let out a weepy chuckle. How could you possibly go on crying when you were being comforted by squirrels?

CHAPTER 13

SpongeBob SquarePants woke Tima up. Her trusty cartoon friend was gurning at her from the glow-in-the-dark face of her yellow alarm clock, beeping insistently, one hand almost on twelve, the other pointing to nine. 11.45 p.m.? She was rattled and confused for a moment. It had been a long time since she'd woken up in the dark to the sound of her alarm. Normally she woke up at 1.34 a.m. on the dot when the beam came through.

And then she remembered why she'd set the alarm. The message!

Just you, please. It's important.

Tima pulled on her usual night gear, listening carefully in case Mum and Dad were still up. A moth flew in from the landing and told her it was OK, they were asleep. She smiled, holding out her palm, and then carefully took it to the window and set it free with a thank you.

Night Speaker. Elena had discovered the legend of the Night Speakers after researching their weird abilities online. Some ancient legend said children might win the gift of fluent communication with wildlife . . . provided their parents were willing to risk leaving them out every night for a week in a wild place while they were just babies. If the babies didn't get eaten, they got the prize. Of course, she had no clue whether the legend applied to *them*—the story dated back centuries. Tima was pretty sure her mum and dad hadn't dumped her in the woods at any time, day or night. But Night Speakers was a cool name and apparently they *could* all speak to wildlife, so it had stuck. They had to call themselves *something*.

Just you, please. It's important.

Tima had some science to back it up, too. She'd had an MRI scan and it was a fact that the language centres in her brain were abnormally enlarged. Maybe all Night Speakers had the same weird brains.

Just you.

All day she had wrestled with whether or not to tell Elena and Matt. She really *wanted* to but the minute she did, she would be ignoring this Carra's plea to go alone. There was no way Matt would let her go alone, even if Elena agreed . . . which was doubtful. Matt seemed to think she was just a child and needed protection. Huh! He seemed to have forgotten how often she had helped save them all from catastrophe, thanks to her insect pals. It was annoying to be the youngest, the smallest, the 'kid'.

No. She would go alone to meet this Carra and then arrive at the bandstand as usual and tell them about it. They'd planned, via text message that day, to sneak out some stuff to mend the hide and make it a proper den. She'd already sorted out a bin bag of cushions and blankets to take. It was stuffed in her wardrobe, along with some scented tea light candles and a string of battery-powered LED lights. She'd need to nip back indoors again after meeting this Carra person, and take the bin bag out with her. Double danger—going in and out twice. And leaving so early was a danger too. Mum and Dad didn't usually go to bed until about 11 p.m.—unless Dad had a dawn shift at the hospital or Mum was needed early at a farm.

She opened the bedroom door and listened. No sound. No light around their bedroom door. Good. Time to go.

There wasn't much moonlight but the pale blue of the streetlamps meant Tima didn't need to pull her torch out of her backpack. Over the road, the grassy area she'd first seen Carra rummaging through was deserted. She wandered across, glancing left and right. Nobody about. The Thornleigh Town Hall clock was chiming as she rested against a tree, safe in the shadows. As it struck twelve she almost expected the strange woman to waft into view like an apparition. But nothing happened. For several minutes Tima waited, silently. Only the whisper of leaves and the contented hum of the night insects filled the dark.

By ten past midnight, she was annoyed. She got little enough sleep—she could have had another hour and a half of it if she'd known Miss Leather Pants wasn't going to show. She shook her head and stepped away from the tree. Maybe she could get a snooze in between now and beam time.

A hand fell upon her shoulder. She spun around, heart lurching, hands raised.

'Sorry to frighten you.' The woman stood there in the shadows. 'I just needed to wait for a bit—to be sure you were on your own.'

'*Really?*' snapped Tima. 'Aren't you a bit old for sneaking around and jumping out on kids?'

'Kids? You don't seem like a kid to me.'

'Well . . . no, maybe I don't,' said Tima. Hadn't she been thinking just the same thing not half an hour ago? 'So . . . what's all this about?'

'I had to be sure,' said Carra, pulling something long and shiny out of her own backpack. 'I thought maybe I had imagined it. You *are* young. Not a kid but—what—seventeen in eye ocean years?'

Tima shook her head, puzzled. The woman sounded quite rational but her words were very odd. Eye ocean?

'And clearly not old enough to remember which tongue to use.'

'Um . . . I have only the one tongue,' pointed out Tima,

beginning to shuffle backwards. 'How many have you got?'

'Well then, I guess your transchip has glitched,' said Carra. 'And you haven't noticed. How long have you been here?'

'About a quarter of an hour,' said Tima, trying to sound calm and steady. This woman was beginning to spook her.

Suddenly, Carra grabbed her arm. 'Look—you've been found out. There's no point in trying to bluff. Listen to yourself! You're bluffing in *eye ocean*! I don't know what you're doing here but I have to act—you know that.' She tapped a small red badge on her lapel, with several gold stars glittering on it. 'It'll go better for you with the Quorat if you surrender now. And tell me where Morto is.'

Tima wrestled her arm away, her heart beating fast. 'I don't know *what* you're talking about! You're not making any sense. Look . . .' Suddenly she thought of Elena's mum, and added, '. . . are you off your medication or something?'

Carra stood up straight, releasing her. 'I have enough medication to get me through. Have you? You can't survive here for long, you must know that. Your lungs aren't fully developed. I can't believe they sent you.'

'Look—I think you've got me mixed up with someone else,' said Tima. 'So—if it's all the same to you, I'm going back to bed now.' She turned away.

'Wait—Tima!'

She spun around. 'How do you know m—?' Something ice-cold punched her in the face and she knew nothing more.

CHAPTER 14

An autumn fog lay low in the valley as Matteus crept out of the flat. He was late. He'd had to text Elena and Tima to say he was on his way. Dad had been up, drinking late into the night, watching an international boxing match and bellowing at the screen. What Dave Wheeler, forty-five, overweight, full of beer and unseen in a gym since he was nineteen, could teach an international heavyweight boxer, Matt wasn't sure—but his dad seemed to think he had all the answers.

Dad *was* strong, though. Car valeting was a very physical business; all the stretching up and over, around and under the grimy bodywork created good core strength. The repetitive scrubbing and waxing motions worked the arm and shoulder muscles. The crouching to clean out wheel arches developed strong calves and thighs. It all made you look pretty gym-fit.

Matt sometimes wondered what the chemicals in the detergents and silicon sprays might be doing to his teenage lungs, though; only today he'd had a coughing fit after finishing a Ford Focus.

Dad would be in good shape too, even for forty-five, if he didn't drink so much. He was certainly fit enough to rough up his son any time he felt the urge—but Matt had managed to avoid any trouble over the fight at school. His bruises were faded enough that he no longer had to put the make-up on. Mum had noticed. She'd touched his face just this morning and looked worried, glancing at her husband as he ate his fried breakfast. Matt had shaken his head slightly. *No. Not him.* And she had visibly relaxed.

It was hard to imagine what Mum had ever seen in him. Dave Wheeler had come to work for her father, Tomasz Kowski, twenty years ago. He'd charmed young Aleksandra, who was only nineteen at the time. Two years later they were married. The wedding photos showed a young, happy couple; Mum, pretty in traditional white, with her dark hair piled up on top of her head and pearls at her throat; Dad, awkward in a shiny suit and a wide grin. Mum didn't talk much about their marriage but he had worked out that the troubles came when the drinking started, not long after Grandpa Tom died and the pressure of running a business fell upon the couple. Such a pathetic story.

Matt had made a decision that he would never drink. Never. A lot of his school mates—er, make that *ex*-school mates—had already tried beer and lager and nicked spirits from their parents' drinks cabinets. He'd been at parties and watched the effect it had on them. It made them loud and stupid and out of control. Three more reasons to stick to his plan. He would drink Coke and tell them there was rum in it. Once he'd added rum essence to a can and convinced Ahmed completely that it was real rum in there. Ahmed had then got 'drunk'. On a teaspoon of cake flavouring.

Idiot.

Matt felt the night wrap around him like a comfort blanket as he headed silently along the street towards the posh end of town where Tima lived. A gentle fluttering above his head made him smile and lift his bunched fist to the sky. Lucky landed on it a second later.

'It's a bit cold and misty for you to be out tonight,' he murmured, stroking her iridescent feathers with one finger. 'But you're a bad-ass bird, aren't you? Out in the dark.'

'Misty,' she replied. 'Bad.'

He noticed her gleaming body was thrumming—as if she'd been flying very hard for some distance to reach him, although she was usually roosting in nearby trees. 'Everything OK, Lucky?' he asked, but before she could reply his phone buzzed in his pocket and he pulled it out to read a text from Elena.

Worried! Tima not at bandstand. No answer to my texts!

Matt frowned. Tima was a demon for texting. Tima not replying within thirty seconds was cause for concern.

He texted back:

Wait thr. We cn chck out her house when I get thr. Probly parents up.

He broke into a run and got to the bandstand just after two-fifteen. Elena was sitting on the wooden balustrade and peering at her phone. She looked up as he arrived and shook her head. 'Something's wrong. I know it.'

Matt led her back to Tima's house. Lucky had been flying, staying with him as he ran, and now she landed again on his fist. 'Lucky,' he whispered, crouching down below the brick wall with Elena. 'Can you fly in to Tima's room? Find out what's happening?'

Lucky flew off immediately to the window above the large Victorian porch over Tima's front door. Tima's window was ajar and, after landing on the sill, Lucky disappeared into the room. Matt and Elena stood up, watching anxiously, waiting for their friend's face to appear at the window. Maybe she'd send a message back with Lucky. Lucky might come out and say, 'My phone's broken and Mum and Dad are downstairs!' in an exact copy of Tima's voice. Lucky flew back to them seconds later. When she opened her mouth Tima's voice did not echo out of it. It was her own, high pitched tone, and she said only two words. Again.

'Misty. Bad.'

CHAPTER 15

'I've taken her blood.'

Tima twitched in her sleep. Something wasn't right.

'. . . appears to be eye ocean age seventeen or eighteen and is probably already permanently damaged. Whoever buddied her across is beneath contempt.'

Tima drifted in and out of sleep, wondering who was talking. Had she left a radio app running on her phone? She lifted her head from her pillow and then realized it wasn't a pillow. It was a tree root. She shot up into a sitting position and gave a small shriek when she discovered her wrists and ankles were bound together by some kind of sticky netting. Something sticky was also on her face, stinging the skin beneath her left cheekbone.

'Keep still,' said her captor, a short distance away. They were in a cave of branches. Carra's face was lit by a pale lilac glow, emanating from a device on her wrist which she seemed to have been speaking into.

'You *attacked* me,' mumbled Tima incredulously.

'I disabled you, temporarily,' she said. 'I needed your blood.'

Tima gaped. 'My *blood*?' Oh great. Another vampire in town.

'If you cooperate with me,' went on Carra, 'you'll live a lot longer.'

'What . . . you turn me into one of you . . . and I get to be undead for eternity?' Tima squeaked. 'No thanks.' She wished she'd got a cross and chain to wear, like Elena. She'd teased Elena about her crucifix and now it looked like a vampire was about to get the last laugh.

Carra wasn't laughing though, or lunging for her throat just yet. She sat, cross-legged, and surveyed her captive calmly. 'You won't last much longer without me,' she said. 'You need to get back to Ayot. I'll take you home as soon as you tell me who your accomplice is—and where.'

'What? You're not making any sense!' said Tima, panic now racing through her as she tried to tug her wrists apart. 'I haven't got an accomplice! What is it you think I've done?'

'I don't know what you've done,' she said. 'But I know you shouldn't be here. The fact that you *are* here is breaking the law and I can only imagine there's a criminal reason for it. I know what you eye oceans are like. I've brought your kind in before. Wherever you show up, it's bad news for the natives.'

'Why—why do you keep saying *eye ocean*?' Tima gasped, still straining at her bonds.

Carra pressed a small yellow orb on to the ground,

uplighting the waxy leaves of the large shrub they were camped under. She turned, fixed her dark eyes on Tima's, and let out a long sigh. 'This idiot gameplay is getting a bit wearying. If you're not from Ayot, why are we speaking Ayotian?'

Tima drew breath, and then opened and closed her mouth a few times, baffled. 'I'm speaking *English*,' she said, finally. 'So are you.'

'No,' said Carra. 'I *was* speaking English when we first met—and then I said something in my own language, Targanese, which you instantly responded to in Targanese. I followed it up with a few more phrases, to be sure—and you were quite fluent. Then I switched to Ayotian and you were *completely* fluent. This means you're either from Targa, which I know you aren't, or from Ayot, which I know you are. So let's cut the play acting, shall we? We're both speaking fluent Ayotian and the game is up, Tima. Where is Morto? It *is* Morto, isn't it, who brought you through?'

Tima suddenly realized something with complete clarity. She had been captured by an insane person. Someone who was completely deluded. Looking at the woman's beautiful face in the dim glow, she could see how earnest she was—how much *she* believed her mad ramblings. Tima understood then that nothing she said or did would convince this woman that she wasn't from Targa or Ayot or flippin' Krypton, if that's what she'd made up her mind to believe. Nothing would stop her helping herself to an eleven-year-old girl's blood supply, either, if she'd decided to be a vampire.

'My wrists and ankles hurt,' Tima groaned. 'Can you please undo them? I won't run away.'

Carra raised her eyebrows. 'Seriously?'

Tima took a long breath and let it out. 'OK, then. But I have to warn you, if you don't release me, I have friends who will hurt you.'

Carra looked around her. 'Do you? Friends who will hurt me as much as they're hurting you? Tell me—has the weakness begun? The dizziness? The blackouts? The nosebleeds? Did Morto warn you about those when he brought you through?'

'I don't know who this Morto *is*!' yelled Tima, giving in to fear and fury. 'Let me GO! Or you *will* be hurt!'

But Carra turned away and began fiddling with her pack again. Tima felt a coolness wash over her. A decision. It was time. Her friends were poised to attack—they only needed a word from her.

Tima lay back down on the ground, closed her eyes, and said: 'Yes. Please.'

At first she heard just a few gasps and slaps and then yelps of pain. Then scrabbling—panicky scrabbling. The midges and mosquitoes had come in on the first wave—biting and stinging any exposed skin they could find. Ants, too, marching across the woodland floor and climbing into Carra's boots to sink their strong jaws into her ankle flesh.

Tima felt her heart race, thrilled and horrified in equal measure. She was lying here, apparently helpless, but she had more help than this woman could possibly know.

Next came the spiders, dropping from the twigs and leaves; false widows and tube webs and black lace weavers. This was the point at which Carra began to yelp. She probably thought British spiders couldn't bite. She was wrong.

'Release me,' Tima called out. 'Or it'll get worse.'

Carra scrabbled through her backpack and began to unearth some kind of can which she started to shake. Insecticide? Oh no! Tima couldn't allow that. 'OK—you asked for it,' she said. And then she called out 'YES! GO AHEAD!'

The wasps arrived in a small cloud and after the first couple of stings, her captor was yelling with pain, snatching up her bag, fighting her way out of the branches and running for her life.

JUST CHASE! Tima called after her striped champions. *Only sting if she turns back. As soon as she's half a mile away, leave her alone.*

The angry buzzing and the crashing through the undergrowth as her foe escaped slowly grew fainter until she couldn't hear either sound at all. Tima lay still, sent out a *thank you*, and then wondered what she was going to do next. She was helpless. Her wrists and feet were completely gummed together by the weird rubbery mesh. And she had no idea where she was. She didn't even know what time it was. She could have been here all night. The yellow orb thing seemed to have gone along with the woman's bag. The remaining light filtering in through the leaves was still pretty feeble; she was some way from dawn. Another stab of panic hit her. What would happen if she wasn't back in bed and Mum or Dad came in?

She had to get a message to Elena and Matt . . . but she couldn't even tell them where she was. Oh wait. Of *course* she could tell them. *She* didn't *need* to know. The insects would tell them; they would put up a big swirly beacon above her so her friends could see exactly where she was.

86

BUT . . . . if she called Matt and Elena to her, they might stumble right into the path of Mad Leather Chick and get a faceful of *go to sleep glue*. Even as she was trying to work out what best to do, she felt a gentle tickle on her wrists and ankles. She peered down and just about made out a chain of ants working their way across the white gummy mesh. They were biting it! Gnawing through it! Hundreds of them.

'You little heroes!' she marvelled. 'Can you get through it?' It might take a while. She would have to be patient. But more and more ants were now swarming across her bonds; she could even *hear* the chomping as their strong, sharp jaws lacerated the mesh. It took five minutes before she was free. Then she had to sit tight for a couple of minutes, allowing her six-legged heroes to get clear of their work, so she wouldn't crush any of them as she finally got to her feet. She sat still and rubbed her wrist and ankle joints, easing the blood flow back through them, and eventually got up and staggered out into the open air.

She turned slowly, getting her bearings. She appeared to be on the side of a hill. It rose up behind her, covered in thin wiry grass with occasional patches of white. Further down it she could make out more bushes, scrub, and trees. It looked familiar. She realized it was the far side of Leigh Hill. On the other side it fell away in a chalky cliff face—the remains of an old quarry site which now housed Quarry End industrial estate. This side was left to its own devices as a wildlife reserve. In other words, the local council pretty much ignored it.

And if she wasn't mistaken—she was about five minutes' scramble away from the new Night Speaker clubhouse.

She pulled her mobile out of her jeans pocket and instantly saw the stack of increasingly panicky texts from Elena. It was 2.54 a.m. They would have been trying to reach her for well over an hour now. With trembling thumbs she tapped out:

I'm OK. Just got kidnapped. Free now. Meet me @ hide as soon as u can. Don't call. Just txt. Shhh. Kidnapper still at large.

CHAPTER 16

Spin sat four or five metres up in an elm tree, catching his breath. The fight had been easy. Fun. Some guy in a hoodie, intent on breaking into an off-licence round the back. Dark alley. No bulb in the security light. Perfect.

In his earlier days, he'd considered wearing a cape; a classic, red silk-lined job that would really tick all the boxes. But he soon realized that a cape was **a.** ridiculous and **b.** very awkward. He often needed to climb, run, and flip at great speed and a cape would get caught, flap about stupidly, probably strangle him. Also, someone might think he was styling himself on Batman which would be nauseating. OK—so the Dark Knight and he had a few things in common, but *he* wasn't out at night for the sake of humanity. He was out for the sake of Spin. It had occurred to him that his work might very well be keeping the crime rate around Thornleigh down, but that was by the by. No. Caped crusading was not his thing.

So he'd opted for the black silk coat instead. With red lining. Ah come *on*! Why not?

Yes, tonight's entertainment had gone well and his prey had been very obliging. Spin ran his tongue across his pointed canines and grinned. But his breathing shouldn't still be laboured. He'd been back on one of his favourite roosts for nearly ten minutes, replaying the scene in the alley behind the off-licence, yet his heart was still jogging along quite fast. Was he out of shape? He took several long, deep breaths, but didn't feel much better. Maybe tonight's prey was on drugs and he'd somehow ingested something.

There was buzzing. Spin sat up on his branch, cocking his head, listening hard. He was familiar with every noise the night made and this was . . . unusual. Few night-shift insects in Britain buzzed like that. That sounded more like . . .

'WASPS!' he yelped and then grabbed his black cowl and pulled it over his head just as the swarm arrived, thousands of small, winged bodies pelting past him through the darkness. What were wasps doing out at this hour? Spin had only seen a night-time swarm like this once before, and frankly, that wasn't a night he wanted to remember.

Through the sound of the high-pitched angry droning came crashing and gasping just below him. Spin peered down through a gap in his cowl and saw a figure lurching through the trees. It sank down to the woodland floor and pulled itself into a ball, whimpering. This must be the unfortunate who had stumbled into the wasps' nest in the dark. Bad luck.

Worse luck for him, too, if the hapless wasp-botherer was going to collapse just under his tree. The swarm didn't look like giving up any time soon and *he* was just as likely to get stung now as the real target of their annoyance.

But suddenly the buzzing dropped in intensity and then it evaporated altogether. Soon, all he could hear were the groans of the person below. Spin pushed back the cowl and flicked on a wrist light, sending a pale red glow downward. It was a woman. And—if he recognized those leather boots correctly—it was *the* woman. His jogging heartbeat picked up to a light sprint. Oho! *This* was turning out to be his night after all. His attacker was down there, whimpering beneath his feet.

He descended silently and landed beside her, allowing a twig to snap under his foot to attract her attention.

Blearily, through a curtain of tangled dark hair, she looked up at him. His sprinting heart stood still for a moment. She was a pitiful sight. Her face was a mass of stings; eyes just slits between swollen lids, hands smothered in livid red bumps.

'Oh my,' said Spin. 'We *have* been in the wars, haven't we?'

The woman said nothing. Perhaps her tongue had been stung too. Maybe she was having an allergic reaction and about to expire right here and now. Oddly, although she had it coming after attacking him, he didn't want that.

'I've heard the stung-to-death look is all the rage on the Paris catwalks right now,' he said. 'But it really doesn't suit you.'

She gave a grunt and attempted to roll her eyes.

'I think *you* may need a trip to the hospital,' he said. She shook her head violently. *Interesting.* 'Oh, but they get so *bored* at this hour! It's just drunk after drunk. They'll be delighted to have *you* and all your angry boils!'

She tried to get up but then sagged under the weight of her backpack. She was defenceless. But truth be told, defenceless had never appealed to him. He liked a little fight back and she'd promised a *lot* of fightback in their next encounter. It was disappointing. Spin sighed. This really wasn't his style but if he didn't get her to A & E soon she might be properly dead by the morning. And properly dead people were no fun *at all*.

Spin shook his head, glad nobody could see this. He leant down and hauled her up by her armpits. She whimpered again. 'Come on, Waspy Wendy, work with me here.'

Getting her to walk was difficult; she was barely conscious and her breathing was quite laboured. For the last five minutes he had to carry her, slung across his shoulder. He was glad of all the training. Saving severely stung women had never been in his mind as he worked out and practised his martial arts for hours, but whatever. He tried to get her to drop her backpack but she held on to it fiercely, and mugging wasn't his style so he let her keep it, even though it weighed her—and therefore him—down quite a bit.

The small emergency unit of Thornleigh General Hospital was brightly lit but quiet; only one ambulance was waiting outside and its driver and paramedic were leaning against the vehicle, drinking tea and chatting. Glancing left and right, Spin carried the semi-conscious woman to the far side of the ambulance, deposited her and her bag on the ground, banged loudly on the side of the van, and then sprinted away into the darkness before he was seen.

He heard them find her and go into action as he walked away under cover of trees. His heart was still jogging along and he felt quite light-headed. Well, that's what being a hero did for you. He really shouldn't make a habit of it. It was peculiarly satisfying, though. He couldn't wait to find her again once she had recovered. She'd be in his debt. He was going to be *so damn cool.*

Heart was still pumping though. He remembered it had been a bit elevated before the wasps came. Unease crept back in through his good mood. It was well before dawn, but Spin decided it was time to go home.

CHAPTER 17

'Why did you go alone?' demanded Matt. 'That was such a stupid thing to do.'

Tima stared at him, still picking sticky stuff off her wrists. 'I'm not *stupid*,' she snapped. 'I knew it was risky. But if I'd taken both of you along with me she might never have shown up and I'd never have found out . . .'

'What? What *did* you find out then?' Matt raised his arms, let them drop, and then bounced agitatedly on his heels on the wooden floor of the hide.

'That she's very probably *insane*,' muttered Tima. 'And now, very definitely *in pain*.'

Elena felt a pang of worry. 'How—how badly do you think she got stung?'

'I don't know,' said Tima. 'I told the wasps not to sting her unless she came back. So if she just kept running away then she will have been fine. I called them off after a few minutes.'

'But,' Elena said, taking a breath, 'if she was being stung she might not have known *which* direction she was running in.'

Tima flung her hands up. 'So, *what*—are you telling me I should have just stayed there—tied up—waiting for her to drink my blood?!'

'You should never have gone to meet her on your own in the first place!' snapped Matt. 'That's what we're telling you! Then you wouldn't have got kidnapped, would you? How could you be so dumb? Especially after what she did to that stupid vampire wannabe. And yeah, thanks for finally telling me about that.' He glared at Elena.

'Look—can we just calm down a bit?' Elena said. 'Have some cocoa?' She slipped her backpack off and pulled a tall flask out of it and three tin mugs. They said nothing, still simmering with annoyance, but when she poured out three mugfuls, they each took one, and buried their noses in the chocolatey steam with a grunt of thanks. She pulled out some digestive biscuits too and they settled on the floor and ate them hungrily.

'Look, we're all tired and shocked,' said Elena, after a couple of minutes. 'We were really freaked out when we knew you were missing, Tee.' She touched Tima lightly on the head. 'Lucky went into your room and came back to let us know you were gone. We didn't know what to do. I don't blame you for calling in the wasps. I would probably have done the same, but, look—Matt's got a point. I think we should always let each other know about anything which happens in the dark hours. We're a team, aren't we?'

Tima nodded, compressing her lips. 'OK,' she said. 'I get it. I feel stupid, that's all. Makes me bad-tempered. And now you've made me worried. I mean, she kidnapped me and stuck my wrists and ankles together—but I didn't want her badly hurt. I hope she isn't. I hope she's just scared off and won't try anything like that again.'

'I can send Lucky to find out,' said Matt. 'She can ask the owls.'

Tima looked up at him with a pained smile. 'Yeah. That would be good. Check she's not going into some allergic reaction or anything.'

Matt called Lucky down from her roost in the branch that was hanging through the hole in the roof. He stroked her head as she perched on his hand and then she flew out through the trapdoor, message received.

'So . . . tell us what this Carra woman said. Tell us all of it,' said Elena. Tima related the weird conversation she'd had.

'She kept saying I was an eye ocean,' said Tima. 'Said I was *speaking* eye ocean. What's that supposed to mean? And she talked about a place called Ayot.'

'So . . . did she mean you were from this Ayot place?' asked Elena. 'So . . . an Ayotian? Like—Egypt and Egyptian?'

'Maybe,' said Tima, nibbling thoughtfully on her biscuit. 'And she seemed to think I was lying to her about living here in Thornleigh. She kept asking about another one; someone else who had "brought me through". Said I was too young to be here. She also said I would get sick . . . feel dizzy and have nosebleeds . . . if I didn't go back with her.'

'And she threatened to drink your blood?' asked Matt.

'Well, actually, no. She said she had to *take* my blood,' said Tima. 'But if she did it while I was conked out I can't see any sign of it. I can't feel any punctures or anything.' She checked her neck and then her inner elbows and wrists.

'If she hadn't already attacked Spin, I'd think she was maybe another . . . one like him,' said Elena. 'So if she's not . . . then, what is she? Do you think she's just . . . ?'

'Nuts,' said Tima. 'She's nuts.'

Elena felt herself stiffen. 'Mentally ill,' she corrected, quietly. She noticed Matt glaring at Tima again, but this time it was to spare *her* feelings.

'Oh God, sorry,' said Tima. 'I didn't mean . . . I mean, your mum isn't anything like *her*.'

'If she is mentally ill, then she needs help,' said Elena. 'Whether she's been badly stung or not. I think we need to find her.'

Lucky flew in right on cue, landed on Matt's shoulder and said, in an exact copy of Elena's worried voice, 'Find her.'

'Have you found her?' asked Matt. 'Where is she?'

'Found her,' said Lucky, now sounding more like Matt.

'Is she nearby?' asked Matt. Lucky twitched her head and shook her feathers. 'OK,' said Matt. 'Take us.'

Following Lucky through the woods wasn't easy; it was still some way before dawn and very dark. They had to use their torches to avoid tripping over roots or getting twigs in their faces. But soon Lucky led them back to the lights of the town and a steep embankment which led down to the brightly lit concrete in front of Thornleigh General Hospital. They paused, hidden among straggly shrubs and small trees, and stared down.

'She's gone to A & E,' breathed Tima. She looked stricken.

Elena squeezed her shoulder, secretly glad that Tima was affected like this. Sometimes she worried that the younger girl didn't fully understand the power she had. 'Good,' said Elena. 'She's in the right place. They'll give her something for the stings and probably get a mental health nurse or doctor along to see her too, especially if she keeps saying the kind of things she was saying to you.'

'Should we report her properly?' asked Tima. 'You know . . . in case she tries to kidnap anyone else?'

Elena and Matt were silent. Eventually Matt said what Elena was thinking. 'If we do we might as well wave goodbye to our Night Speakers time, to the den, to . . . all this. I mean, I might still get away with getting out at nights sometimes. I'm older. But you and Elena? Elena's mum really doesn't need this—and *you'll* be grounded for years. You know you will.'

Elena shivered. The thought of Mum finding out was bad enough, but if the authorities got to know about her nights on the town . . . well, the social services would helicopter in and start asking all kinds of questions, and what might happen next was unthinkable.

'Let's set up a watch,' said Tima. 'Ask our friends to watch out for her for the next twenty-four hours. They can tell us if she comes out of there. Tell us where she is . . . do you think?'

'It's worth a try,' said Matt. He checked his watch. 'It's getting late. Time to go back and try to sleep. You first, Lucky.'

He blew gently on the bird's feathers and Lucky flew away to her roost. 'Tomorrow night we can sort out the den. And maybe get some information about where this woman is. If she's out again we'll go and confront her. Together. Yeah?'

Tima and Elena nodded. 'Yes,' said Tima. 'Together.'

CHAPTER 18

Carra came to as they were injecting her with something. She resisted the urge to punch them all out of the way and run for it. She was struggling to breathe and guessed that whatever they had just shot into her veins couldn't make the situation any worse. In fact, within a couple of minutes, it had definitely made things better. The tightness in her chest and throat eased off and the intense pain of the stings dropped to a low throb.

Adrenaline. Of course. And antihistamine. Some painkiller too. It was risky to take this medicine—but maybe riskier *not* to take it. Her own meds weren't designed with stinging Earth insects in mind. She lay back and pretended to be unconscious while they fussed around. A man and a woman, both in tunics, were tending to her, occasionally patting her cheek and trying to get her to talk.

She moaned a little and then burbled something in her own language. Neither of them understood it but one of them suggested she might be Polish. 'I think Janina is on duty,' said the woman, writing something on a chart on the end of the trolley bed Carra lay on. 'See if you can find her. If this one *is* Polish she can translate.'

Then she turned to Carra and gently touched her swollen face. 'You'll be OK,' she said. 'The painkillers will kick in soon.' The young doctor clearly understood that tone of voice could convey a lot. Carra was touched. She wanted to say thanks but more than that, she wanted to get out of here. If they started rummaging through her backpack for clues to her identity, things could get very awkward. She needed to seize her moment to run; wait until they'd wandered off to see to someone else in the busy emergency department.

Eventually the doctor wandered around to the patient in the next cubicle. An old man, by the sound of it, wheezing and coughing.

'Was down my allotment,' she heard him say, in between gasps. 'Came over all funny. Breathless, like.'

'Have you any history of asthma?' asked the doctor. 'Bronchitis?'

'Nope. Been fit as a flea for the last seventy years,' puffed the old man. 'I get out to my allotment in all weathers, I do— never had a problem. I think . . . it's the power station, that's what I think. They reckoned there was a gas leak, didn't they . . . when the chimney went up in flames? How do we know it's not leaking again, eh?' He paused to cough violently and then added,

'You never know what's in the air around power stations. I blame the government.'

Carra's own breathing was better now, and the pain and swelling on her face and hands was receding. She felt stronger. She sat up quietly on the trolley and saw her backpack on a chair nearby. She was close to a short corridor which led to the main reception area. Being dumped by the ambulance in such a state had got her a free pass directly into the treatment room. This meant the reception staff probably hadn't seen her come in—so if she just walked out again now, they might not notice her.

She got to her feet, swayed a little, light-headed. She reached into her backpack and retrieved her inhaler—took a couple of quiet gasps from it—felt her breathing and her brain function improve further. Then she stood very still, sensing everyone nearby in the building. Her path to the exit was clear. Behind the curtain the old man was still coughing and talking about gas leaks and the doctor was checking his chest.

Three, two, one . . . GO.

She didn't run. She grabbed her backpack, slung it over one shoulder, and walked silently and swiftly along the polished vinyl flooring, out on to the corridor, on towards the heavy double doors to the reception area. Pushing through them she saw at least a dozen people sitting around waiting to be seen and two stressed-looking receptionists dealing with some argumentative men, clearly the worse for drink. She kept her head down and crossed to the exit, drawing little attention.

Outside, dawn was just beginning to creep across the eastern sky. She walked past two ambulances, across to a steep bank and the blessed relief of darkness under bushes and trees. From here she had only to walk deeper into the woods.

She wondered whether she would again encounter the pale-haired young man she'd shot the other night. That he had taken her to hospital was baffling. That he hadn't stolen her bag was more baffling still. But bafflement had been her chief state ever since she'd arrived here. For now, she just had to get back to her camp, rest, and recover. Tomorrow she could work out what to do about a junior Ayotian who seemed to have learnt to control insects. Could there be anything more dangerous than an Ayotian with a superpower?

The next time she saw Tima, she would have no choice but to kill her.

CHAPTER 19

Tima felt all the air leave her lungs. She could not breathe. Pushing a last thin squeak out of her throat, she stared into her foe's face and wondered how the hell this had happened.

'Aaaaand—BREATHE!'

Mr James chuckled as Tima and Lily spluttered and dragged in oxygen as if they'd been under water for the past two minutes.

'That was impressive,' said the music teacher, checking his watch. 'You held that note for four seconds longer this time. Your diaphragm control is improving. It's amazing what practice can do. I have asthma, you know, but I've done so much breathing practice over the years, I hardly ever need to use an inhaler. The lungs are like muscles—you can train them.'

'I've been practising,' Lily gasped. 'Every day.'

Tima didn't speak. She was busy filling her lungs again. *She* hadn't practised at all. She'd had no time to even *think* about practising. All weekend she'd been obsessing about Carra by day and working on the Night Speakers den with Matt and Elena by night. The insects had told her, around teatime on Saturday, that Carra was no longer in their territory. Later, Matt said Lucky confirmed this and Elena reported that the squirrels had seen Carra track down through to the south-western end of the wood and then disappear. Where she'd gone, Tima had no clue. Maybe the mothership had beamed her up.

Now back at school on Monday, she was still coming to terms with the fact that she had to work so closely with Lily. Lily—who had toiled so hard to make Tima feel like an outcast from the moment she'd arrived at Prince William Prep. Lily, who was jealous of Tima's better voice. Lily, who whispered to her friends and snickered whenever Tima was nearby.

Of course, Lily was never *obviously* horrible to her—she was too clever for that. She hid her poison in sweet words, always careful to give an impression to the teachers that she was caring and considerate. Well, Mr James wasn't totally taken in, Tima knew that at least. But he still wanted them to sing together—maybe he was trying to get them to put the past behind them and be friends.

'Tima! Are you OK? You look almost *purple*!' giggled Lily. 'Is this all a bit too much for you?'

'No—I'm fine,' said Tima. She wasn't great, if she was honest with herself. Working on the den was so much fun they had been losing track of time and getting home later. Matt and Elena had stapled some thick plastic across the window to cut out the cold and they'd cleaned all the dead leaves out with the dustpan and brush Tima had borrowed from the utility room. She'd strung up her LED lights and put candles in jars on the windowsill. A rug and some cushions really made it look cosy and Elena had also brought a little wooden chest, which they filled with bottles of water, biscuits, and snacks. Next they were going to get the paraffin heater up there and some planks and nails to mend the roof. It was SO Enid Blyton! Even Matt was loving it. He couldn't hide it, however hard he tried to be cool.

So they'd all got back to bed late last night—and now she was running on about four hours' sleep. She was an idiot. If she kept this up, Mum and Dad would start worrying again and maybe get in the habit of checking in on her in the small hours. Tonight she MUST get as much sleep as possible.

'I've been learning the lyrics in French,' Lily was now saying. Oh *great*. She was showing off, reading the words aloud for Tima's benefit and piling on the accent like she was in a bad play about the Paris resistance.

'*Sur la rive en fleurs*,' she declaimed, holding up the music sheet and glancing at Tima, unable to disguise her triumph. '*Riant au matin . . .*'

Tima sighed. Then she took a breath and gave her rival a bright smile. 'That's brilliant,' she said. 'You really *are* fluent.' She tried to be genuine about it—to make an effort. 'I'd love to speak French like that.'

Lily looked slightly bewildered, glancing from Tima to Mr James, and then back at Tima again. Then, holding the music in front of her and furrowing her brow slightly, she went on: 'Let us descend together. Gently floating on its charming risings; on the river's current.'

'Oh,' said Tima. 'That's nice—but you should stick with the French. It sounds a lot better. Don't you think so, Mr James?'

Now Mr James was staring at her, looking confused. 'Erm . . .' he said. 'You'll have to go a bit slower for me, Tima— I'm not as good as you and Lily. You put me to shame!'

Tima now took *her* turn to furrow her brow. 'I was just saying it sounds nicer in French than in English.'

Lily put down the music and gave her a glare. 'You should have told me you speak French! You didn't say you did,' she snapped, looking really put out.

'But . . . I don't!' Tima was baffled. 'Honestly—I'm really bad at it. Especially all the tenses and past participles and stuff like that. I was probably bottom in our French test yesterday.'

Lily stood still for a moment, narrowing her blue eyes at Tima. 'Well, you seem to be managing OK *today*! We're *both* speaking fluent French right now and you're not having any problem are you? Why didn't you just *say* you could? Why have you always got to try to show me up?!' She slapped the music down on top of the piano and stalked out of the music room.

Tima turned to Mr James, wide-eyed. 'Sir . . . am I . . . am I speaking French?'

But Mr James was staring after Lily. 'What's up with Lily?' he said.

'I don't know . . .' said Tima. 'But . . . are we speaking English now?'

Mr James screwed up his face in confusion and turned back

to her. 'Of *course* we're speaking English now. Tima . . . are you quite all right? What was going on between you and Lily while you were both jabbering away in French? For just a *moment* there I was hoping it might help you get on better, once I heard you both—but evidently not!'

'Sorry,' said Tima, feeling tiredness swoop down on her. 'We just keep winding each other up. I don't know why.'

'OK—well, let's call it a day today,' sighed Mr James, stacking his piano music into a pile. 'Please try and get things straight with Lily, though, will you, Tima? This duet is going to be the top of the bill at the harvest festival. I want to show you off—both of you—and it won't work if you keep arguing with each other. You both need to be more professional.'

Tima nodded and promised she'd try harder. Leaving the building, replaying the conversation she'd just had with Lily, she knew exactly where and when she'd had one just like it.

Lily, in the music room just now: 'We're *both* speaking fluent French right now and you're not having any problem are you?'

Carra, out in the dark four nights ago: 'We're both speaking fluent Ayotian and the game is up, Tima.'

She found Lily in reception, gathering her bag, hat, and blazer. 'Lily,' she said, leaning against the massive Portland stone fireplace that dominated the entrance hall. 'I'm sorry. I wasn't trying to show you up. I really didn't think I was that good at French.'

Lily peered at her suspiciously. 'You're just weird, do you know that, Tima? Really weird.'

'Yeah, I know,' said Tima. She was too tired to argue and,

frankly, she *was* weird. If Lily knew exactly *how* weird, she'd probably be screaming all the way down the sweeping gravel drive of Prince William Prep. 'Mr James said we have to try to be . . . more professional. Try to make this work.'

Lily stood up straight, her blazer on and her bag over her shoulder. Outside, a huge dark-red 4x4 was pulling up; Lily's mum—blonde and stylish—was calling to her. 'OK,' Lily said, unsmiling. 'I can be professional if you can. I'll talk to Mummy about getting you over for a practice.'

And she stalked away.

Tima's mum would be here soon. She gathered her bag, blazer, and hat and went to sit on the stone wall outside. She was so tired. *So* tired. So much stuff was tumbling through her mind—some good and some bad—it felt as if her brain was being mangled. She made a mental list in no particular order:

1. The Night Speakers had a new den!
2. She'd been kidnapped a few nights ago . . .
3. Yeah, but the den!
4. She'd probably badly wounded her attacker with a swarm of wasps . . . she might never know for sure.
5. She was going to sing a brilliant duet!
6. With *Lily Fry*.
7. She seemed to have suddenly become a fluent French speaker without even trying.
8. Did that mean her kidnapper really *had* been speaking Ayotian after all? And so had she? And if so . . . what the hell?

Mum pulled up in the Merc and Tima stumbled into it. 'Mum,' she mumbled, 'can I have a really big bit of cake when we get home? And then can I fall asleep in front of some cartoons?'

CHAPTER 20

'They're all dead. Every single one of them.'

'It is a virus, I think.'

Matt sat in the tall grass at the edge of the school playing field, biding his time. If he hadn't glanced out of the window in the science block stairwell at just the right moment, he wouldn't have seen the danger. But luck—or rather Lucky—was on his side. He'd clattered out of Biology with twenty-eight other kids, funnelling down the stairs to join the crowds heading to the lockers to get their stuff and go home, and as he'd passed the tall window which looked on to the street below, there'd been a sudden, sharp click on the glass. He glanced up and saw a starling swooping away from the window—downwards. That's when the curiously shaved head of Liam Bassiter came into view for a few seconds, on the far side of the school fence.

Matt knew Liam wasn't back in school yet and there was only one reason he could think of that the boy would be skulking around outside. Payback.

So instead of joining all the others and heading home, he'd hung back, got all his stuff and then gone down to the field to sit quietly for a while, thinking about the events of the last few nights and wondering where this mysterious Carra woman had got to. The animals reported only that she'd left their territory. They'd probably never see her again. He wished he could never see Liam Bassiter again either. He reckoned Liam would give up and go home after about half an hour—he wouldn't want to be caught loitering around by the teachers once they finished work and started heading home.

Matt knew if Liam was alone he could take him at any time. It was only his promise to the head teacher that made him take the option of hanging back and avoiding the confrontation. And now he was listening in on a conversation with Mr Rosen and Mr Janssen as they wandered past on the way back from the school's kitchen garden. It sounded like a something from a zombie movie.

'The whole tank—wiped out in one weekend,' went on Mr Rosen.

'Once one gets a virus, they all get it,' replied Mr Janssen. 'It is quite common.'

The head teacher sighed as he paused by the concrete steps that led up to the school, just out of sight of Matt's lurking place on the other side of some bushes. 'It was like fishy Armageddon. I've had deaths in the tank before, but nothing like this. I should do a test on the water.'

'Yes, the water,' said Mr Janssen. 'I expect it's the water.'

'Anyway,' said Mr Rosen, with a brisk inhalation. 'Glad to see your project is going so well. Your orchids have had lots of admiration in my office. Got any more? We could sell them for the school; raise some funds.'

'That is a good idea,' said Mr Janssen, and Matt could hear that he was smiling. 'I am making more.'

'Excellent. When might they be ready for a table sale?' asked Mr Rosen.

'Any day,' said Mr Janssen.

Mr Rosen said goodbye and headed up the steps, puffing. 'I really must get fitter!' he called back down to Mr Janssen. 'I've never been so out of shape!'

Mr Janssen didn't reply but Matt could sense that he was still standing at the foot of the steps. The man murmured something quietly in his own language. Then there was a thick silence. Matt kept very still, sensing no movement from the gardener. Was he just waiting there, staring into space? Or was he peering through the clump of straggly bushes and wondering what Matt was doing there? At last he heard the man grunt and move away, back towards his plastic tunnels and greenhouse and rows of marrows.

A thud on his shoulder told him Lucky had arrived. 'Lucky . . . that man. That gardener,' said Matt. 'Do you think he's a bit strange?'

Lucky flew up, turned a circle in the air and dropped back on to his shoulder. 'Strange,' she said. He'd have known that she agreed with him, even if she'd said nothing at all. Their

113

communication was very instinctive these days; a kind of telepathy. It was the starling's habit to mimic, though, and Lucky seemed to enjoy speaking bits of his language. So he enjoyed talking aloud to her too.

Matt checked his watch. He'd been here for nearly twenty minutes now. There would be dirty cars waiting for him at home. Dad would be getting angry. But . . . another ten minutes should see Liam off. He got up and wandered across the field towards Mr Janssen's domain, Lucky still riding on his shoulder. He still had time to kill and he was curious.

'Bad misty,' said Lucky suddenly, in his ear.

'No mist now,' said Matt. Sometimes Lucky could be quite random in the things she said and he wasn't sure she exactly understood the words she was parroting. He could pick up only a vague sense of misty swirls from their deeper, non-verbal level of communication.

Mr Janssen was nowhere to be seen as he arrived at the wooden picket fence surrounding the kitchen garden. Matt opened the gate, stepped inside, and wandered along the vegetable patch to the greenhouse. He paused, peering through the slightly steamy glass. He couldn't see Mr Janssen here either. He should call hello and make his presence known.

But instead he pushed open the lightweight door and stepped into the greenhouse. It was a building of aluminium and glass—about the length of a bus—with a low roof, only a few inches above his head. Plants and seedlings were laid out in rows on wooden benches along the middle and on thinner shelves at the sides, leaving a path around the central bench. Bags of compost and peat and assorted tools lay around, and two thirds of the way along there was a partition of thick, clear plastic, sectioning off an area beyond.

A riot of colour shone through, wobbly and translucent, like an impressionist painting. The room beyond was filled with blooms, similar to those in Mr Rosen's office. Matt walked quietly to the vinyl partition, Lucky's claws suddenly gripping hard through his school jumper. He pushed the curtain of heavy plastic aside.

The flowers were spectacular; large and thick with curling petals of every colour, from white and yellow to pink and red. Their centres were a deep-purple shade with stamens of black, dusted with orange pollen. They stood high on thick, bamboo-like stems with many dark-green leaves edged in orange. Scattered down the stems were strange globular things—also dark green with a purple star shape at the top. They made him think of sea urchins, clinging, oddly, to a land plant. Maybe they were buds, getting ready to flower.

He realized he'd stepped inside fully when the curtain sighed shut behind him. The air was thick with scent. It was sweet but also . . . strangely *musty* . . . *cheesy*, almost. It caught in the back of his throat.

'They're pretty cool, aren't they?' he asked Lucky. Then he realized she wasn't on his shoulder any more. When he glanced around and down he saw her on the floor, turning a slow circle in a fine layer of dirt.

He dropped to his knees and scooped her up into his hands, feeling suddenly very tired. He got to his feet and backed out of the flower room, taking Lucky with him. Her heart was thrumming under his fingers.

Outside she seemed to rally and was soon up on his shoulder again as he walked wearily back across the school field. 'You and me,' Matt said to her. 'We *have* to get some sleep tonight.'

CHAPTER 21

Mum was outside when Elena got home, working on the pond. There was no pump or fountain now, after Elena had returned them for the refund, but there were a couple of crates with waterweed floating up out of them; the cheaper plants which she'd felt they could just about afford.

Over the weekend, fitting out the new den with Matt and Tima, she'd been careful to only use up a *little* of the food and drink from home. They'd all sat around, enjoying her hot chocolate and biscuits, and then she was immensely relieved when Tima opened her bag and got out some lemonade and a big multipack of crisps. She was glad she wasn't expected to be 'mother' when it came to the food. She really couldn't afford it.

They had benefits coming through each month and a small amount from Dad, by standing order. Elena had no idea where her father was these days and only the regular modest payment told her he was even alive. At Christmas and on her birthday he sent a card with a few scrawled lines and some huge Xs as if to make up for the all the fatherly love she'd missed out on for the past three years. There was usually some money too.

But mostly they got little in the way of extra cash; just enough for the bills and the household stuff and a small mobile phone for each of them. Mum's big brother, Uncle Philip, also sent money from time to time, to help keep his sister and niece afloat. Elena's new school uniform and shoes had been covered by Uncle Philip. She was trying very hard not to grow out of them.

Mum was humming as she crawled around the edges of the pond, pinning down the rubbery black liner with chunks of limestone and chalk which Elena had helped her collect from the edges of the old quarry yesterday.

'Looking good,' said Elena.

Mum sat back on her ankles and surveyed her work critically. 'It's not bad. It needs to bed in a bit. It'll take a few weeks to look natural. The rock looks good, doesn't it? It's hard work, though!' She stood up and Elena saw that she was quite pink in the face. She coughed and scrubbed her hand through her messy fair hair, leaving some leaves in it.

Elena eyed her mother closely. She seemed calmer today. Hopefully the meds were kicking in now. 'Want some tea?'

'Yeah—I'll be in soon. Just need to do a bit of weeding over there,' said Mum, waving towards an overgrown border near the fence. 'I have to keep checking what's growing there. There's

Japanese knotweed a few doors down, you know.' She narrowed her eyes.

'Um . . . is there?' said Elena.

'You don't know what that is, do you?' said Mum, heading for the border, shaking her head. 'It's a *nightmare*. It's so invasive that it's actually *illegal* to knowingly let it grow in your garden. It's like the cockroach of the plant world—gets everywhere and is almost impossible to kill. I swear it must have been dropped here by an alien species.'

'How do you get rid of it?' asked Elena, leaning in the kitchen doorway. She really must try to get more sleep tonight. After the dramas of last week, the anxiety about where the kidnapper woman might be (nowhere near them now, according to the squirrels), and the doing up of the den, she was seriously in need of some more zeds.

'You *don't* get rid of it,' said Mum. 'You pay men in white overalls to come and remove it and disinfect the ground. It costs a fortune. Which is why it'd better not spread into *this* garden.'

She came in a couple of minutes after the tea was poured out, collapsing on to the sofa and gratefully cupping a mug in her hands. She took a long drink and then gave a couple of dry coughs into the steam.

'Are you getting a cold or something?' Elena peered at her.

'Maybe,' sighed Mum. 'Or it's just the autumn damp getting to me. Feels like the air's kind of murky. Oh, season of mists and mellow murkiness . . .' She chuckled and Elena relaxed. It really did look like Mum was coming down from the mania. As long as she didn't slide down *too* far and get low, things might be a bit easier for a while now.

Her phone burred and she plucked it out of her pocket. A text message from Tima:

News from flies! Carra back in woods! Do u think we shd try to find her tonight?

Elena sighed. So much for a restful night. She texted back:

Maybe. She might need help. All three of us together, though.

Tima responded:

OK. BTW had weird thing at school today. Call me?

Elena promised to phone in the next half hour, and after putting some potatoes in the oven to bake and persuading Mum to take a shower, she went to her room, flopped on to the bed, and called Tima.

'Right, so I was in music with Lily Fry,' said Tima, the moment she picked up the call.

'Hello to you too!' said Elena.

'What? Oh—yeah—hi—but listen. Lily was showing off, reading out the French lyrics to the "Flower Duet". And I understood them. All of them.'

Elena rolled on to her front, kicking her school shoes off on to the floor. 'Erm . . . OK. Good for you.'

'No—you don't understand,' said Tima, impatiently. 'I am *rubbish* at French. Really bad. Could never be bothered with it. But this time, I was getting it *all* and that's not the freakiest bit.'

'Go on,' said Elena, suddenly feeling her skin prickle.

'I just started talking to her . . . in French,' went on Tima. 'And it was so easy I didn't even know it *was* French until Lily started getting all annoyed about it. She thought I'd been winding her up and pretending to be bad at it. But, Ellie, I *swear*, I've always been *terrible* at languages. I can't even speak that much Arabic and both my parents are Arab!'

'Wait, hold on,' said Elena, sitting up. 'Are you saying you just started to understand her, even though she was speaking another language?

'Yes! It was so . . . easy. I didn't even know I was doing it. Mr James was there and he said he could hear both of us jabbering away in French like a pair of natives.'

Elena was silent for a moment, remembering something.

'Elena? Are you there?' Tima's voice rang out of her phone.

'Yeah,' said Elena. 'I'm just thinking. Um . . . I think I might have done the same thing.'

'What? Where? When?'

'Yesterday . . . I was picking up some meds for Mum at the pharmacy and Mrs Patel was there, chatting to her son. And normally she chats away to him in . . . I don't know—Urdu? Hindi? But this time she was talking to him in English. At least I *thought* she was. And then she started saying this stuff— this . . . *personal* stuff about me and Mum . . . and my dad. I was really shocked that she'd say things like that right in front of me.

She wasn't saying anything really horrible—just the kind of stuff you say about someone when they're not around. You know—kind of blunt. And when she looked up and saw my face she looked so freaked out. She wasn't expecting me to understand a word of what she'd said . . . because . . . I think . . . she wasn't speaking English. But I did understand it. I *did*.'

Now Tima was silent for a few beats and then she said: 'Remember the MRI scan I had back in the summer? They told me then that the language centres in my brain were way bigger than normal. You remember?'

'Yeah. I do,' said Elena, now awash with goosebumps as she began to understand.

'Well—yours and Matt's will be the same,' said Tima. 'It stands to reason—we're all in the path of the beam and we've all been affected. So . . . we can communicate with animals and understand them. And now I think we're starting to communicate and understand *humans* too—humans whose language we never understood before. We're . . . what is it? Multilingual.'

'Wow,' said Elena. 'That's just . . . wow!'

'Oh, come on—it's WAY more wow to be able to talk to animals!' said Tima. 'But this is also really cool. We have to check Matt! We'll try him out tonight—while we're on our way to find Carra. It explains so much! Why I understood *her* language too. I thought she was just a crackpot, you know, telling me she was speaking another language while she was speaking English—but now . . . maybe she really *was* speaking Ayotian or whatever it was.'

'Does that make her any safer?' asked Elena.

'I don't know,' said Tima. 'I guess we'll find out tonight.'

CHAPTER 22

The road was empty of students—and Liam Bassiter—when
Matt finally reached the school gates. He breathed a sigh of
relief. Lucky flew away; she knew he no longer had a problem.
He let her go. She needed to rest. It did worry him that he
was messing with her birdy rhythms, keeping her up at night.
Starlings normally roosted at dusk and didn't get up until dawn.
He also worried that she was a colony bird and he was luring her
away from her colony too much.

He paused, watching her become a speck in the sky. Then,
just as he was shrugging his bag up on to one shoulder, he felt
a hand clap heavily on the other. He spun around in shock,
ready for a punch—only to find it wasn't Liam. Or any of
Liam's gang.

It was the gardener. He was staring down with those

unsettling, pale eyes and carrying a cardboard box. 'You like my flowers, yes?' he said.

Matt didn't know how to respond. He just stared, feeling his skin getting hot under the man's icy glare.

'I see you go in and look,' said Mr Janssen. Matt couldn't tell whether he was angry or pleased. 'You go in and you spy on my work, yes?'

'I—um—yeah. Sorry. I . . . I was just . . .'

'Interested,' completed Mr Janssen. He nodded and his face moved weirdly and Matt realized he was attempting a smile.

Then he thrust the box into Matt's arms. In it was one of the exotic plants from the greenhouse. 'Take it,' said Mr Janssen. Matt stared at the white blossoms. Mr Janssen shrugged. 'Give it to your mother.' And then he walked away, back into the school grounds.

'Thank you . . .' Matt stared after him and then shook his head. Life was just full of surprises.

Dad gave him a baleful look across the bonnet of a Subaru as he arrived home but the look changed to suspicious curiosity as he noticed the cardboard box.

'Sorry I'm late,' said Matt, quickly. 'The head teacher's been getting me to help out with the school garden. And look—this is what the gardener gave me to give to Mum!'

His father put down his chamois leather and strode over, wiping his hands on his overalls. He took the box and peered into it. 'Hmmm,' he said. 'Flowers.' He raised his thick eyebrows and peered hard at Matt while Matt tried to work out what could possibly be *wrong* with flowers for his mum. Dad was clearly trying to work out the same thing and must have given up because in the end all he said was, 'Well—take them in to her, then. And make it quick. You've got work to do.'

Mum had her back to him in the kitchen when he arrived. She was on the phone to her cousin Weronika, back in Warsaw. Mum spent some hours every week talking to her cousin and a couple of other relatives back in the old country. Matt had been taken to meet them, along with Dad and his brother Ben, many years ago, when he was about six. He had vague memories of strange meat stews and lots of singing in an old, dark house near a field. Mum was always saying they should go back again but Dad would always squash her plans, pointing out that they couldn't afford the air fare.

Matt quietly pulled the plant out of the box and placed it on the table. It was set into an ordinary, brown plastic pot but it still looked impressive, with its tall, green, segmented stems and their little sea-urchin blobs—and those luxurious white blooms with the deep purple centres. He hung around, waiting for Mum to turn and see, earwigging absently on her chat with Weronika.

'. . . has been pretty good. Yes—football season—all is well with the world. Yes. No. No—not for a while. I think . . . I think it's getting better and Matt is coping well. I know. I know—but there's nothing else I can do, is there? A help group? As if! He would never go. Never . . . No, don't say that. It's OK. It's not that bad.'

She turned and saw him, smiled and rolled her eyes in a 'sorry, I'm on the phone' way and then went on: 'He's just got back now. He's a good boy. He gets into these fights and sometimes I think he sneaks out at nights but he's a good boy.'

'I *don't* sneak out at nights!' he blurted, panicked into lying. What had she *seen*?!

Mum spun around to stare at him, looking surprised. Then she just waved him away and finished the call rapidly, before turning back and noticing the plant. She was delighted with it. 'It's beautiful! What is it?'

'Erm . . . some kind of orchid?' Matt shrugged.

'The stems are wrong for an orchid,' said Mum. 'Orchids usually have very woody stems, thick oval leaves, and silvery roots that reach up into the air. This is . . . like a bamboo. How do I take care of it?'

'Oh,' said Matt. He hadn't thought to ask. 'I don't know. The school gardener grows them—he gave me this because I helped him out the other day. I'll have to ask him what you do with it.'

'For now, it's going here,' said Mum. She found a saucer and placed the plant on it, right in the centre of the deep, tiled windowsill, improving the view over the moss-encrusted top of the car-wash canopy. 'It will brighten my day every time I have to wash up! Thank you, Matt!'

She gave him a hug and even though he was too old for mum-hugs he was still pleased. It was lovely to see her smile. 'What I was saying to Aunt Weronika,' she murmured in his ear. 'You heard me?' She pulled back and looked at him searchingly. 'In Polish?'

'Oh—I didn't really hear much,' he said. 'You know me—lazy with my Polish.'

'Just . . . shhh. You know?' she said. He nodded. Like he was going to say anything to *Dad*.

She hugged him again.

'Enough of that, Mummy's Boy,' grunted Dad from the doorway. 'You've got cars to scrub.'

CHAPTER 23

They abandoned mending the den roof that night and instead set out to find Carra. Tima's insects had been backed up by word from the squirrels. The woman was still in the woods.

'She hasn't moved for a long time,' said Elena. There was fear in her voice; she couldn't help it. The squirrels were very clear on where this woman was but less clear about what state she was in. Could she be dead? Could she have wandered around for three days and finally come back into their patch and collapsed?

'She's just asleep,' said Matt. 'She's set up camp. That's all.'

Tima didn't say anything as they made their way up the hillside by the light of their narrow torch beams. Elena knew she was worried—and guilty. There wasn't any real reason why she *should* feel guilty. After all, the woman *had* kidnapped her, tied her up, threatened her . . . but a swarm of wasps was pretty heavy weaponry. It was a bit 'sting first, ask questions later'.

As they scrambled down the other side of the hill towards the trees, Elena could make out a glittering beacon of insects, guiding them to their destination as clearly as the arrow on a satnav. The woman wouldn't know the beacon was there. They had all asked their animal accomplices to keep their distance. The most she might have seen was some squirrels darting through the branches overhead; she'd have no idea they were spies.

They fell quiet as they entered the thick darkness of the wood; even Lucky rode in silence on Matt's shoulder. The floor was thick with leaves and needles, and hardly made a sound underfoot. As they got closer to her camp, Elena felt the hairs on her neck and shoulders begin to prickle. And then Tima whispered: 'Can you hear that?'

There was a faint hiss in the air—almost like rainfall—but steadier. And now Elena could see a soft light through the trees. As they grew closer, Elena felt her throat constrict. The woman lay against the wide base of a mature fir tree, her head resting on her bag. She was motionless. 'Hey!' called out Elena. She did not respond. *Oh God. Don't let her be dead.*

Tima made a whimpering noise. 'I didn't mean it!' She ran abruptly towards her kidnapper and then something utterly unexpected happened. She rebounded.

She actually *rebounded*.

She appeared to have smashed into an invisible barrier. Like something from a madcap TV sports show, she made a *thwump* noise, squeaked with shock and flipped backwards on to the woodland floor, doing an almost perfect reverse roll and landing by Matt's feet, gaping upwards in shock.

'What the—?' Matt said.

Elena felt the tingling get stronger. 'She's . . . she's got a force field!' she murmured, disbelief ringing through her words. She'd never believed there were *real* force fields. Tima was getting up now, clearly not hurt, so Elena walked slowly forward, holding out her palms. At the same point where Tima had rebounded, her skin met with a curious sensation—both hot and cold and fizzing with energy. It was repelling her hands, the way magnets repel each other when you put positive to positive. 'Wow!' Elena breathed. Then she looked beyond her thrumming, splayed fingers and saw the woman was looking right back at her. 'Oh, thank God!' she breathed. 'We thought you were dead!'

'Who are you?' said the woman. Her voice sounded strong enough.

'My name's Elena—and that's Matt and, well, you've already met Tima.' The other two were at her side now, also carefully touching the invisible barrier and looking amazed in the pale lilac light emanating from somewhere within the force field. There was a camp, Elena could see—a groundsheet of some kind and a pot of something that might be food.

'Why are you here?'

'We were worried,' Elena went on. 'I mean—you shouldn't have kidnapped Tima, obviously—and she had no choice. She had to defend herself. She just, maybe, overdid it a bit with the wasps.' Elena winced as she looked at the woman's face. Elena was betting it had looked a lot worse four days ago, but it was pretty bad even now—covered in pink lumps. She took the tube of insect bite cream from her pocket. 'If you let me in, I can help. A bit.' She held up the cream.

'If I let you in, I let *anything* in,' said the woman. 'Stinging things. Biting things. I have to protect myself.'

'I know,' said Elena. 'I don't blame you. But, look, you're not the only one who's freaked out here. I mean . . . you did kidnap Tima and try to drink her blood.'

The woman made an explosive noise. 'I did *not* try to drink *anyone's* blood!'

'You said!' Tima suddenly spoke out, hotly. 'You said you wanted my blood!'

'I did,' Carra replied. 'And I've already *got* it.' She pulled a slim glass phial out of a pocket in her bag and waved its ruby contents in the light. 'While you were unconscious. I didn't want to *drink* it—I wanted to *test* it.'

'Why?' asked Matt, baffled.

'Do you know who your little friend is, boy?' asked Carra, pushing herself up to a sitting position.

'Ye-es,' said Matt, narrowing his eyes. 'But I don't know *you.*'

Carra let out a long sigh. 'Look,' said Elena. 'Why don't you let me in? I've got cream for your stings—painkillers too. Have you had anything since you left the hospital? I bet you haven't.'

The woman stared at Elena for a long time and then reached into her bag. 'You can come in,' she said. 'All three of you. But nothing else. None of her . . . little friends.' She glared at Tima.

She retrieved a small, silvery triangle with a blue light blinking at the top, rested it between two dark pine roots, and pressed something on it. At once, the prickly skin sensation stopped and the hiss left Elena's ears.

'Be careful,' said Matt.

Elena walked over and knelt close to the woman. She uncapped the tube of cream and put a liberal blob across her fingers. 'I'll be gentle,' she said, in a voice she recognized from bad nights with Mum. Then she began to dab the cream on the woman's face; working it softly across the stings, which felt stony and hot, even now. How bad must it have been when it first happened? 'How's that?'

The woman sighed and nodded. 'Better. Thank you.'

Elena sensed Matt and Tima coming in closer and sitting down, watching. 'You've got some cool tech,' she said, putting more cream on the back of the woman's hands. 'It's Carra, isn't it?'

'Yes,' said Carra.

'How does it work? The force field?'

'Too difficult to explain,' murmured Carra.

'OK—so explain this. Why did you want to test Tima's blood?'

There was a pause and then Carra answered: 'She only arrived in your lives recently, yes? Around . . . I don't know . . . May or June time?'

Elena glanced back at Tima and Matt, shrugging. 'We all met and became friends in May,' she said.

'Yes, I thought so. And . . . you never knew her before?'

'No,' said Elena. 'Her family only moved here late last year. From London. What's your point?'

'Tima isn't from London,' said Carra.

'Her *parents* are from Yemen,' said Elena. 'But Tima was born in London! She's as British as Matt and me.'

'I'm actually half Polish,' added Matt. 'Born in Britain, though.'

'She isn't from Britain or from Yemen,' said Carra. 'She's not from this planet.'

Elena looked back at Tima who was raising her palms up in an elaborate shrug. 'You see? Barmy!'

'She's from a planet called Ayot,' went on Carra. 'And she is here to annihilate your people.'

Elena put the lid back on the tube of cream and used her best, calmest, voice. 'Carra—what makes you think that?'

There was a sudden prickling sensation and a hissing sound. Matt and Tima shouted out and Elena spun around to see them patting against the inner curve of a pale lilac dome.

'The force field!' yelled Tima. 'It's back on!'

'That's right,' said Carra. 'It's back on. Nothing can get out and nothing can get in. Your insects can't reach me here, Tima, and your friends are about to find out the truth about you. I might be able to let them go—but you . . .' She gave a regretful sigh. 'I can't let you out alive.'

CHAPTER 24

Spin was late to the party. He'd been doing a high-level lurk above the bandstand where the Can't Sleep, Won't Sleep Club usually met but they hadn't shown up at the usual time. No big deal. It wasn't as if he depended on *them* for entertainment. Most of their talk was about mind-numbingly boring stuff anyway. *Ya-de-ya-de-ya . . . I can control insects . . . ya-de-ya-de-ya . . . Get me, I can speak to squirrels . . . ya-de-ya-de-ya, I'm the bird whisperer, aren't I the guy? . . . Ya-de-ya-de-ya, we're the Night Speakers!* Yes. They'd even made up a name for themselves, like The Secret Seven. It was hilarious.

OK—so they had some freaky superpower stuff going on; but they were still lame. Still strolling around through his territory. Still way less respectful of *his* set of superpowers than they should be. And yeah—he did quite enjoy winding up Elena. She was the *best* to mess with, maybe because they'd been through some scary stuff together. It gave him an in. He walked the line of friend and foe with Elena with exquisite delicacy. He liked to watch the annoyance, confusion, and fascination in those big blue eyes; it's why he'd gone to talk to her about the woman who'd shot him.

He hadn't expected her to be all emotional about something. Stuff was going on in that house of hers; something to do with her mum, he reckoned. One day he'd find out.

The woman who'd shot him was also on his mind as he dropped silently on to the conical roof of the bandstand, slid down it, and landed like a gymnast on the grass. He didn't know what had happened to her after he'd dumped her next to the ambulance and now he was cursing himself for not taking her bag. He *should* have taken her bag. Not because he was a thief—that really wasn't his style—but because if he'd kept her bag she would have been forced to seek him out again once she was recovered, to get it back. Then they could get round two underway.

And without the weaponry in that bag at her disposal, he could have had some very decent sparring.

Where was she now? Probably patched up and moved on to a ward. Maybe a psych ward—she clearly had some issues.

He felt twitchy and bored. He decided to check out the spot where he'd found her, covered in stings, in case she'd left anything else in the vicinity while she was being chased across the woods beyond Leigh Hill. And it was only as he'd slipped deeper into the comforting, inky folds of air beneath the thick tree cover, that it came to him what he was *most* annoyed about.

He hadn't thought to ask. He hadn't thought to say to her: 'Woah! Wait a minute! Have *you* by any chance annoyed a pint-sized girl in dance shoes, with a kick-ass attitude?' Because the last time he'd seen a wasp swarm, it was Tima who'd organized it. Only *that* time nobody had been stung. Had Tima stepped up from being a Night Speaker to some dark entomological assassin? Damn! He couldn't deny it. That was very cool. He would give a lot to be able to command swarms of stinging insects.

He wasn't sure Elena would approve of her little friend stinging people nearly to death, though. That was going to be an interesting conversation to have when he next caught up with the Wide Awake Club.

He arrived back at the tree where he'd found the woman stung to a pulp. He stood and listened. Nothing. Nobody about. But here was *something*. Something bright, half-hidden in the leaves by a tree root. He picked it up. It was a round metal box, a bit like the powder compacts he'd seen women use occasionally. He flicked it open but there was no mirror or powder in it. Just some fuzzy white material which smelt faintly citrusy.

He snapped it shut, put it in his pocket, and moved on, wandering the dark paths he knew so well. And before long, through the darkness, he was picking up noise. Some urgent discussion—a shout—a weird hissing.

Spin stepped out from behind a clump of holly trees to see his favourite three antagonists *AND* Waspy Wendy—all together. Score! Weirder still, they were all under some kind of shimmering, lilac-coloured dome—shouting and waving; like a not-very-peaceful-scene in a snow globe.

The first words he made out came from the woman.

'I don't want to kill her, but once you understand, you won't stop me.'

'Hey!' he shouted. 'Is this a private party or do I get a vote on who gets killed, too?'

There was silence inside the snow globe. Everyone stared round at him.

'*You!*' breathed the woman, who looked a little less deformed and dying than she had last time.

'No, really, don't thank me.' He leant against the smooth bark of a mountain ash tree, folded his arms, and grinned. 'And don't let me stop you. You were about to kill someone? Which one? Elena? No. She's way too well behaved. She probably brought you a cake. Matt? Hmm. Who wouldn't want to shoot *that* face? But still . . . no . . . I can see it's the titchy one you've got an issue with.' He pouted and sang out: 'Aaaaaw—did the nasty little girl try to have you stung to death?'

'Spin!' hissed Elena, who was trying to push Tima behind her—despite Tima's angry struggles to be free. 'You're really not helping! This woman seems to think Tima's a psychotic alien planning to wipe out the human race!'

Spin guffawed. 'Well, you can't blame her for wondering. The kid's got a powerful temper on her.'

'Oh, for God's sake—*tell her*! If you know her, *tell* her Tima's just an ordinary girl like me!'

'Ordinary!' snorted Spin. 'What . . . a Night Speaker? Are you telling me you're ordinary?'

'Why did you save my life?' Suddenly the woman was on her feet. 'I shot you and disabled you. You were going to attack me. And then you show up and . . . take me to get medical help.'

Spin shrugged. 'It's better than staying home and watching *Strictly Come Dancing*.'

He got the pleasure of seeing Elena and Matt blink in surprise. *Ha*.

'Tell me what you know about this girl,' said the woman, pointing at Tima and narrowing her eyes at him. 'Do you know she's Ayotian?'

'I keep telling you!' yelled Tima. 'I am *not* from the planet Ayot! Look . . .' She escaped Elena and Matt's restraining arms and stood right in front of the woman, holding her hands palm up. 'Spin's right. We're *not* normal kids. We're Night Speakers. That means we know languages . . . lots of languages. Instinctively. We only have to hear a little bit and then we understand and can speak fluently right away. Try me! Try me on any language you know!'

Matt looked from Tima to Elena and murmured. 'What's she on about?'

Elena said: 'Speak Polish to me and I'll show you.'

Matt screwed up his dumb face and then said: 'I don't know much. How about this . . .' And then he began to jabber away in what could have been any Eastern European language as far as Spin was concerned.

Elena started joining in. Matt looked amazed. Meanwhile, over on the other side of the snow globe, Tima and Waspy Wendy were now speaking another language entirely which sounded not unlike Icelandic with a touch of Klingon.

Spin felt laughter gurgling up through his throat. His boring night had taken SUCH a turn for the better.

The woman suddenly yelled: 'STOP!' She sank down on to the ground, exhausted. 'Everybody! Listen! This is important. Let me get this . . . You can all speak other languages . . . *including* the languages of *wild animals*. Is this what you're telling me?'

'Yes,' said Elena, grabbing Tima and pulling her back to the edge of the hissing lilac dome.

The woman frowned, creasing her inflamed brow. 'When did this start?'

'About four months ago,' said Matt. 'Just after we began waking up at night.'

The woman looked up at him sharply. 'What was waking you up?'

'We don't know exactly what it is,' said Matt. 'But it comes through at 1.34 a.m. every night. It's a kind of sound . . . like a song. It travels on a sort of beam. The beam goes through my bedroom—and Elena's and Tima's. It always wakes us up.'

'Can you remember the date . . . the date it started?' demanded the woman, looking around them all with great intensity, pulling a skinny blue canister out of her bag.

'That better not be a weapon,' yelled Matt. 'Because even if you shoot us all dead, sooner or later you'll have to come out of this thing and our friends will be waiting for you.'

The starling on his shoulder flapped its wings madly and yelled, 'Waiting for you!'

Spin felt the night air suddenly charge with living things. Insects hung in the air and swarmed the roots and earth. Owls swooped low over the hissing dome. Three foxes and two badgers loped into view and the leaves overhead began to shake with squirrels. He pressed himself back against the tree but none of the creatures took an interest in him.

Meanwhile the Wide Awake Club was having difficulty in remembering when it had all begun, so he sighed, cupped his hands around his mouth and yelled: 'First week of MAY.'

Once again the woman stared across at him, startled. 'The first week of May?' she said, staring through the curve of filmy lilac towards him. 'You're sure of this?'

'Well, May the fourth was the *first* time I saw Mona Lisa here staring out of her bedroom window.'

Elena was now peering over to him. 'The *first* time? How many nights were you were watching me?!'

He shrugged. 'You know me. I like to lurk.'

'The beam first woke me at one thirty-four on the first night of May,' said Tima. 'I remember because we had our first dress rehearsal that day.'

'Oh, dear mountains of green,' murmured the woman, closing her eyes. 'It's a bi-post beam. Tima, I'm sorry.' She held up a phial of rather beautiful blood.

'Don't get any ideas, freak,' muttered Matt, shooting Spin a dark look.

'I didn't get as far as testing this. I lost some of my gear while I was running from the swarm,' said Carra.

Spin held up the round metal box. 'This, perchance?'

'Yes,' she said, narrowing her eyes. 'Throw it to me.'

He swung it in his fingers, considering, and then threw it. This whole thing was too interesting for games. It shot towards the lilac dome and a tiny hole appeared, allowing the small missile through, closing instantly once it had passed. The woman caught the metal box in one hand, flipping open its lid and revealing the fluffy white stuff. She tipped a ruby drop on to it and the blood spread like a rose, glowing brightly for a few seconds before turning blue. The woman snapped the lid on it shut, dropped it to the ground, and then buried her face in her hands, groaning something in another language. The others all looked at each other wide-eyed.

'Well, don't leave me out of the punchline!' wailed Spin. 'I'm in this story too. What is she saying?'

Elena glanced over at him. 'Tima's not an alien. She gets to live.'

CHAPTER 25

'It's not much . . . but it's home,' chirruped Tima, as they settled
Carra down on some cushions and a sleeping bag.

'I still think it was *stupid* letting *him* know where it is,'
muttered Matt, glaring into the corner where Spin was leaning
up against the wooden wall, examining his black-varnished talons.
'D'you get those done at Nancy's Nail Bar in town?' he sneered.
Lucky, on his shoulder, echoed: 'Nail bar?' like a comedy sidekick.

Spin made a meaningful signal at Matt with one of those
manicured nails. 'No. They grow this way naturally,' he said.
Tima wasn't sure whether he was serious or not. 'And do you
really think I didn't already know about your little den?' He
snorted derisively.

'Look, he was helpful,' said Elena, 'Getting Carra to
hospital.'

'I never shot to kill, you know,' Carra said to Spin. 'Just to stun you; get you out of the way. I left you on your side, safe from choking.'

'S'all right Waspy Wendy,' he replied. 'It's all a game.'

'It's really not,' she sighed, and Tima knew then that she had a lot more to tell them.

It was a good thing they'd worked on the den. The thick plastic across the window cut out the draught, so it was quite warm. Elena got out her flask again and poured out some cocoa while Tima raided the chest for biscuits.

'Is *he* staying for this?' Matt looked balefully at Spin, who was sitting against the wall.

'He's part of it,' said Elena, handing Spin some cocoa. 'There's no point pretending he isn't.'

'Why, Elena, that's the nicest thing you've ever said about me,' said Spin, helping himself to a shortbread finger from the packet Tima had just opened.

'Normal food?' sneered Matt. 'Not just blood then?'

Spin grinned across at him, fangs on show. 'I like to mix it up a bit on a Tuesday.'

Tima watched as Carra tasted some hot chocolate with a wary look on her face. 'Go on—it'll do you good,' she said.

Carra rolled her eyes like an Earth teenager, but took another sip and then nodded. 'It is good,' she said. 'We have something similar on Targa.'

'OK,' said Tima. 'Are you *really* from another planet? If so— where's your spaceship? Wait!' She sat up straight, excited. 'Is that what started the beam? Does it come from your spaceship?'

'No,' said Carra. She took another gulp of cocoa and then continued: 'I didn't arrive in a spaceship. But the way I *did* arrive *is* closely connected with this beam.' She glanced around at them all. 'I am a marshal for the Quorat—a group of civilized planets. It's my job to track rogue travellers who are using cleftonique corridors without permission and getting on to protected planets.'

'Using corridors without permission?' Matt wrinkled his face. 'Sounds like we're back at Harcourt High!'

'A cleftonique corridor is an interdimensional route between worlds,' explained Carra. 'I think you might know it as it a wormhole. It allows us to travel in seconds something which would take hundreds—even thousands—of years to travel in a spaceship.'

Tima felt her jaw drop and sensed the others doing much the same. 'Seriously?' she murmured. She hadn't yet decided whether Carra was the real deal. The force field bubble—which Carra had shut down as soon as they'd all reassured their animal friends she didn't need attacking—was quite convincing, but even so . . .

'But there shouldn't be a corridor to this planet,' Carra went on. 'Whoever has set one up is breaking the law. I found out about it and followed him through.'

'These corridors . . . you mean you can make one and just show up anywhere?' asked Matt, a mug between his palms, staring hard at their guest.

'Not anywhere—the location has to be right. A natural

formation of some kind, with the right geology—and obviously a place where the natives aren't going to see you arrive. It's usually a cave in a fairly remote area.'

'Where is the cave?' asked Tima, glancing around at the others.

'I'm not able to tell you,' said Carra.

'Who is this person who made it?' asked Elena.

'He's an Ayotian,' said Carra. 'Travellers from the planet Ayot are almost always bad news. His name is Morto and he's here, on your planet. Maybe even in your town. And he's not here for the food and the scenery.'

'Hang on—wait a minute,' said Tima. 'You said this . . . corridor thing . . . it's connected with what's been happening to us? How?'

'The corridor is created with a beam of energy—and this must have somehow travelled beyond the access point. That's what is disturbing your sleep.' Carra drained the last of her hot chocolate. 'My information shows that Morto came through on the first of May. According to Tima, that's when you started waking up. It's no coincidence.'

'And the . . . Night Speaking?' asked Elena. 'That comes from this beam too? This corridor?'

'It must be. The beam is an enhancement energy which helps corridor travellers to quickly learn alien languages. I don't know exactly how, right now, but it's out in your world, travelling in a kind of loop. And, as you say, it travels right through your bedrooms. That's the best sense I can make of it. Although . . .' Carra glanced around at them all. 'I have *never* heard of it

enabling anyone to speak to animal life. That's new. That's . . .
amazing.'

'You're telling me,' muttered Matt

'Night Speakers,' murmured Carra. Her face softened as she
let the words sink in. 'It's really . . . quite something.'

'So . . . if *I* get myself into the path of this beam every
night,' said Spin, making Tima jump again—*seriously*, she
sometimes wondered if he even *breathed*! 'Would *I* get this
animal-control thing? Or the language thing?'

Carra shook her head. 'I don't think so. I think you would
have needed to be there when the first surge of energy came
through.'

'But,' Spin began.

Matt spun around and glared at him. 'You're not one of us,
freak,' he hissed. 'Deal with it.'

'He's not a Night Speaker?' queried Carra, looking at Spin,
puzzled. 'Then why is he out at night?'

There was an awkward silence.

Matt gave a derisive snort. 'He thinks he's a vampire.'

Seconds later Matt was airborne. He was thrown bodily
towards the gap in the ceiling. The next moment he was hanging
upside down from the intruding branch, Lucky flapping around
him, squawking in panic. Spin's black silk coat whipped above
them and then there was a punch of displaced air, a billow of
black smoke . . . and he was gone.

For a few seconds Tima, Elena, and Carra stared upwards,
open-mouthed as Matt dangled, clutching at his neck.

'He's *bitten* me,' he gasped. 'I'm going to kill him.'

CHAPTER 26

'It was the stupid aerial on Dad's stupid old radio.' Matt awkwardly held his chin up so Mum could put some Savlon on the wounds.

'You managed to fall on it *twice*?' asked Mum, peering at him over a pad of cold, damp cotton wool, perplexed.

Matt shrugged. He couldn't think of anything else to say; he was so tired, and still so incredibly angry. He hadn't got any sleep at all. Making up the story about slipping on some wax in the car wash and falling against Dad's big, ancient radio with its broken aerial was the best he could do.

He'd been out cleaning cars since 6.30 a.m., working on autopilot as he relived the scene from last night over and over. He refused to believe it. Spin was NOT a vampire. It wasn't true. He was just a freak with a few tricks. Pretty impressive tricks,

Matt had to admit. And a lot of physical strength. Matt was easily the same weight as Spin but that hadn't seemed to be any problem. As Elena and Tima had helped him get back down, shaking, to the floor, what hurt him far more than his injury or even his damaged pride was another emotion altogether.

Jealousy.

He was *jealous* of Spin's strength and speed and confidence. The knowledge burnt inside him far more painfully than the sting of the punctures on his throat. That it had happened in front of Elena and Tima made it several times worse. He'd shoved away their fuss and concern as soon as he'd got his wits back. And then he'd run out to find Spin and smash his face into a pulp . . . and not found him, of course. Elena and Tima and the alien woman hadn't tried to follow him. Only Lucky came after him, flitting from tree to tree as he raged through the woodland, eventually landing on his shoulder when he'd calmed down. She repeated several of the names he muttered for Spin, supportively.

Back at home he'd crept into the bathroom and cleaned up the blood; there wasn't much. Had that freak actually *drunk* some of it? He shivered. There were worried texts from Elena and Tima and several unanswered calls. He ignored them. He couldn't begin to deal with texts or calls. Or mad ideas from alien women. Were they really meant to believe all that interdimensional corridor stuff? And that some alien outlaw was roaming their town? *Really?!* It was insane. But . . . he'd experienced that force field first-hand and that was *right* out of *Star Trek*, wasn't it? He'd lain in bed, staring at the dim ceiling, waves of exhaustion pulling him under, and waves of humiliation and fury dragging him back up. Then the alarm had gone off and it had been car-wash time.

Mum had seen his throat, still scabby and smeared as he came in for breakfast after cleaning a Nissan Micra. She'd insisted on inspecting it and then the questions had come out with the antiseptic.

'It looks like you've been bitten by a vampire!' Mum was saying now, with a snort of amusement.

'Yeah, right,' muttered Matt. 'Can I go now?'

'To school? I don't think you should,' said Mum. 'I think you should go back to bed.'

Matt didn't have the strength to argue—and a part of him wanted nothing more than to sink back under the duvet. But . . . 'What about Dad?' he said. Dad almost *never* let him take a day off school.

'Just go to bed,' she said, glancing out of the window and down to the car wash. 'I'll tell him it's a teacher-training day.'

Matt was awed. Mum had never actually lied for him before . . . as far as he knew. She might have lied without him knowing it, of course, but this was a first—involving *him* in a lie. Siding with him against his father. He narrowed his eyes, staring at her through the fuzz of his unrested brain. She had a look on her face. A determined look. 'Go back to bed,' she said. 'I will wake you up at lunchtime.'

'You'll phone the school?'

'Yes.'

'And Dad will be OK?'

'He won't be putting you to work when you're not well,' she said and there was that determination again, in her voice. Matt felt something inside him swell with emotion. He squeezed it down again and went back to bed. As he drifted towards sleep he could hear Mum in the kitchen, humming and occasionally coughing. And then he thought he heard Dad talking too. Dad didn't sound angry. Maybe he was having a good day.

He felt the plaster on his throat, tugging gently at the broken skin, and the last thought he had before sleep was: 'I'm going to kill Spin.'

CHAPTER 27

There weren't many advantages to having a bipolar mother, but one of them was happening now. Elena had just called the school and told them she couldn't come in until the afternoon because her mum's psychiatrist was visiting and needed her there.

The school believed her. And *that* was the advantage of being a Good Girl. Elena worked hard, handed in her homework on time, didn't make a fuss, kept below the radar. This, combined with her status as a registered Young Carer, meant she was believed. And rarely checked up on.

Mum was actually pretty good today, although a bit wheezy. She seemed to have a bit of a chesty cold but mentally she was good. Not hyper. Not low either. She was sitting at the kitchen table, drawing a rather beautiful (and way too ambitious—for their budget) design for the garden.

'No school uniform today?'

'It's a fundraising thing,' mumbled Elena. Lying to Mum was harder than lying to the school. 'I have to pay them 50p to look this good.' She was in her jeans and sweatshirt and trainers, her backpack slung over one shoulder.

Elena was a Good Girl. Her mum believed her.

She pushed her guilty pangs under as she left the house. This was important. She needed to get back to the den in the woods; check up on Carra and find out more. Carra had important stuff to tell them and last night had been cut short by the dramatic exit Spin had made, leaving Matt dangling and bleeding.

Elena groaned to herself as she walked quickly down the road, in the opposite direction to the school, heading for the hill and the woods beyond. *Spin.* What was she supposed to feel about Spin *now*? She'd just begun to think he might be a sort of friend and now *this*. OK, so Matt *had* been winding him up— telling him he was a freak and not part of their gang—but even so, to throw Matt about like a doll and sink his fangs into him? That was too much. It would probably be better if they never saw Spin again—Matt was so angry there was bound to be a fight. A really bad fight. And Matt would probably come off worse.

Or maybe he'll turn into a vampire too, now that he's been bitten . . .

Elena shook her head impatiently as she climbed up the hillside above Quarry End. Seriously! Spin couldn't *really* be a vampire. That was just ridiculous. Vampires were just a myth. OK . . . so were aliens, maybe, but Carra was clearly the real thing. Spin had never *proved* he was a vampire. All the same, there must be some serious *issues* going on there. Whatever he was, he was dangerous.

And yet . . . he'd carried Carra to hospital. When he could have just drunk her blood. *Look, just stop it! He's not a REAL vampire. There's no such thing!*

Elena went on arguing vigorously with herself all the way to the hide. When she climbed up into it she half expected to find it empty, but Carra was still there. She was sitting up, playing with one of her gadgets, and looking almost normal again. The stings were now just pale pink marks and her skin was regaining its smooth lustre. She had combed her hair and put it into a long plait.

'Oh,' she said, as Elena emerged through the hatch. 'I wasn't sure you were coming back.'

'I said I would,' said Elena. Last night they'd needed to go soon after Matt had raced out, raging into the dark. As desperate as they were to hear more of Carra's story, it was close to dawn and Tima needed to be back in bed before her dad got up for an early shift at the hospital. They'd agreed to put a lid on everything happening in the hide and get back to it today.

'I brought you some breakfast.' Elena pulled a foil-wrapped sandwich out of her bag and handed it over. She also got out a flask, refilled with hot cocoa, as Carra had seemed to like that last night.

'Thank you,' said Carra, opening the foil and peering at the sandwich suspiciously.

'It's cheese,' said Elena. 'I didn't know if you were vegetarian or not.

'Not,' said Carra. She took a bite. 'But this is good. Cheese? What is cheese? I forgot.'

'Um . . . it's fermented cow's milk,' said Elena, wincing slightly. 'Which doesn't sound like anything anyone should ever eat—but we do. And we like it.'

Carra nodded and finished the sandwich before reaching enthusiastically for another mug of cocoa.

'So—um—I took the day off school. Tima wanted to but she can't really. I know Matt would be here too if he could, but he might get chucked out of his school if he bunks off and . . .' She dried up, realizing that all of this meant nothing to a woman from another planet. 'So. What do we need to know?'

'His name is Morto,' said Carra. 'He is here in your world; probably right here in this town. He is making plans. Good plans for him and Ayot. Bad plans for you and Earth.'

Elena gulped. 'What kind of plans? Is he going to bring in an invading army?' Visions from *The War of the Worlds* swam through her mind; flying saucers, death rays, and alien tripods striding across the land, setting fire to things.

Carra gave a dry laugh. 'Armies? Yes. But not the kind you think. Morto is a specialist in warfare of the much smaller kind. His troops don't carry guns.'

Elena gulped again, and sat down on the floor. 'Are you talking about biological warfare?'

Carra nodded, gravely. 'It's not too late,' she said. 'I can find him. I can stop him. I just need to know where he is.'

'Well—haven't you got some gadget in that magic bag of yours which can track him down?' demanded Elena.

'I wish I had,' said Carra, gravely. 'But he has tech of his own—which blocks his traces. I have been searching the town and the surrounding villages and woods and hills for days now.'

'So that's what you were doing when you first met Spin?' said Elena. 'He said you were looking for babies in nurseries—to experiment on.'

Carra pulled a perplexed face. 'Spin . . . He is not a normal boy, is he?'

'No. He definitely is not,' sighed Elena. 'I don't know what came over him last night.'

'He is a predator,' said Carra, simply. 'Beware.'

'Yeah, well, he did probably save your life,' mumbled Elena.

'As the keeper saves game for the hunters,' Carra said. 'For sport.'

Her words chilled Elena. She suspected Carra had just hit the nail on the head about Spin. It was all about the game with him.

'Well—this Morto—what does he look like?'

Carra pulled a small square gadget out of her jacket pocket and flicked it into a glowing screen. A man's face appeared on it. He seemed to be around thirty years old. His hair was fair. His jaw was quite square and his eyes were pale and cold.

'Have you seen him?' asked Carra.

Elena peered at the image, frowning. 'You know, I think I *might* have seen him. I just can't work out *where*.'

'Think hard,' urged Carra.

'Why didn't you just show Spin this?' asked Elena. 'Why *were* you asking about nurseries? Is he going to murder babies?'

'I *would* have shown him this if he had not tried to attack me,' said Carra. 'And no—murdering babies is not Morto's style. Although he *will* murder babies. And their parents. In their millions, if we don't stop him. But I did not mean kindergarten nurseries. I meant nurseries for plants. Morto is a botanist. A grower of plants.'

Elena suddenly stared up at Carra, her heart rate picking up. 'I know who he is,' she breathed. 'And, Carra . . . I know *where* he is!'

CHAPTER 28

Tima was doing OK today. She was managing Lily Fry pretty well.

'You know what?' she said to her least favourite classmate, as Mr James left them for five minutes to go into his office and take a call from reception. 'I think our voices blend really well together.' She wasn't lying, either. Their voices *did* blend really well. Lily had a sharp, cut-glass edge to her singing and Tima had a more mellow sound. The combination of the two actually worked.

'Yes, I think you're right,' said Lily. After a pause, she added: 'And your French pronunciation is pretty good.'

'Thanks,' said Tima. She glanced around the music room, ill at ease with this brittle niceness. 'I wonder what's keeping Mr James.' They both peered down towards the little glass-walled office where Mr James did his desk work and filing. It was hard to see through the glass because there seemed to be a whole load of flowers in the way. Mr James had been talking on his phone extension but now there was no sound. Had he forgotten they were here?

'My mother gave him all those orchids,' said Lily, suddenly. 'She wants him to use them as set-dressing for when we sing the "Flower Duet". You see? Flowers?'

'Yeah. Nice idea,' said Tima, but she wasn't really concentrating. Something was grabbing at her insides, screwing them up. It wasn't the stress of being pleasant to Lily—it was something else.

'She knows the head teacher at Harcourt High and he gave her the orchids,' Lily was prattling on. 'He knows the grower. They're really rare, apparently.'

Tima had actually picked it up on some level from the moment she'd stepped into the music block, but she'd been distracted by Mr James and the singing with Lily. Now she realized, with a sudden thud of certainty, that a serious wrongness was in this place.

There were no insects here. Not one. Unless you included several dead flies on the carpet near Mr James' office. Tima gulped. The last time she'd noticed a building with no insect life in it, things had gone downhill fast. And that weird thing with the disintegrating bee last week . . . she had been so caught up with Night Speakers stuff, she hadn't even thought to mention it to the others. Now it suddenly seemed very significant.

She put down her sheet music and walked towards the office

with its screen of voluptuous orchids. They didn't look like the orchids Mum had at home. They were taller and straighter, on thick green stems like bamboo. Some were white, others cream or gold. All had a deep purple throat with orange-dusted black stamens curling out. Some of the pollen was scattered in drifts against the window. 'Mr James,' she called, aware that Lily was catching up with her. 'Mr James!'

The teacher did not reply. Tima felt sick as she reached the door. The first thing she saw were his brown brogue shoes, tipped upward. He was lying on his back on the dark blue carpet, staring up at the ceiling. There was an orange stain around his nostrils. But worse than this was the trail of foamy stuff dripping out of his mouth and down his cheek and neck.

There was a scream behind her.

'Oh my God!' Lily howled. 'He's dead! He's DEAD!'

CHAPTER 29

It was quiet when Matt woke up. Eerily quiet. He sat up in bed, staring around blearily, then got up and went to his window. Lucky was roosting on the sill. She turned to look at him and said something. It was hard to hear it through the glass but it sounded like, 'Bad mist'. Again. She was getting a bit repetitive, these days.

Matt looked past her, down into the car wash. His watch told him it was 11.13 a.m. . . . and nothing was happening. Dad was nowhere to be seen and there was no soapy water draining across the slanted concrete. Maybe he didn't have any more cars to do today. Matt wrinkled his brow, remembering there had been at least five booked in. Could Dad have done them that fast?

Feeling slightly sick, he opened the window. Lucky flew in and landed on his shoulder, her claws scratchy through his thin

T-shirt. 'Bad mist,' she said, again. Powerful waves of agitation were coming off her, making his skin prickle.

Matt set her down on the open sill. 'Wait here,' he said, and opened his bedroom door. 'Mum. Mum . . . ?'

No answer.

Matt went into the kitchen. He noticed that a petal had fallen from one of the blooms he'd brought home. There was orange pollen scattered across the draining board too.

'Mum . . . ? Dad . . . ?' The sickness wasn't going away. In fact it was getting worse. He didn't think he was going to throw up but his chest felt uncomfortably tight, as if a metal band was squeezing it. He went into the lounge and found the TV was on, with the sound turned down. Outside an ambulance went by, sirens blazing.

Matt arrived at his parents' bedroom door very slowly. As if he was walking under water. He knocked on the door. It was ajar. He pressed it open. Dad was in bed and Mum was on the floor next to the bed. Frothy stuff was coming out of their mouths.

Lucky arrived on his shoulder again.

'Bad mist,' she said.

CHAPTER 30

They heard the sirens before they got out of the woods. 'I think there might have been a big car crash or something,' said Elena. 'That's a lot of sirens.'

Carra gave her a look which she couldn't interpret. 'Hurry,' she said.

Elena wished she'd put on uniform today after all. It would have been easier to sneak into the school grounds with it on— but maybe they'd arrive while everyone was in class and could just creep in around the perimeter.

Four ambulances went past them between the edge of the woods and the school. Elena used her student pass, which was still in her backpack, to unlock the electronic gate and let them both in. The grounds around the sprawling yellow-brick comprehensive were quiet and empty. Happily, no sports team was running around the field. Keeping to the shrubs and bushes at the edge, she led Carra down to the school's new kitchen garden and greenhouse. 'I could be wrong,' she said, eyeing the dark metallic gun at Carra's hip. 'Just . . . make sure.'

'You are not wrong,' said Carra.

'How do you know that?'

'I just know it.'

They pushed open the little wooden gate and threaded their way past the marrows and melons towards the greenhouse. It was difficult to look inside because it was steamed up. Carra moved ahead of her, pushing her back with an outstretched hand. 'Wait!'

But Elena couldn't wait. She had to be sure that she'd done the right thing. What if the new groundsman was completely innocent? What if he was just Mr Janssen, from Holland, like he said he was. She remembered Mr Rosen introducing Mr Janssen during an assembly last term, explaining how the school was going to start growing its own fruit and veg and Mr Janssen would be in charge of the project. Mr Janssen hadn't said much but he'd seemed nice enough. And Matt seemed to think he was OK—hadn't the guy stepped in during the fight and then told the head that it had been five or six boys against one?

The greenhouse door swung shut behind Carra and Elena paused for only a second before grabbing it and following her in.

Inside it was humid. And smelly. Elena gagged and put her hand over her mouth and nose. There were rows and rows of plants in pots . . . and they were all dead. They seemed to have sagged into pools of green sludge and they stank like rotten potatoes.

Carra looked around at the mess, grimacing. Then she stepped through a curtain of plastic to the other side of the greenhouse. Here it couldn't be more different. A riot of blooms, on tall, healthy green stems, filled half of the wooden benches. Judging by the muddy rings on the bare boards of the benches, there had been many more of these plants.

Elena turned to Carra, who was walking slowly around the flowers, her face set like stone.

'Your Morto. This is it . . . isn't it? This is his army.'

Carra nodded. 'You need to get out of here. Stop breathing in now, and get back outside.'

Elena stared at her, frozen with shock. She really had only slightly expected Carra to agree. Carra ran at her and thrust her out past the vinyl curtain, through the chamber of plant death, and back outside to the vegetables and the fresh air.

'What? What are they? What's happening?' Elena garbled, as soon as she reached the outside. 'Did they kill all the other plants?'

Carra nodded, turning back to the greenhouse. 'This is small, now, whatever is already out there. But it's going to be big. Global.'

'What . . . from just a few plants?' Elena couldn't make her brain bend around what Carra was telling her. It refused to understand.

'What we saw in there is a hybrid of the harandela plant,' said Carra, pulling something out of her bag and putting it on the gravel path next to the greenhouse. A cardboard cone. It looked like a small firework; the kind of thing people were going to be buying soon for Guy Fawkes Night. 'The harandela is native to Ayot.'

'You mean . . . he's brought them with him from another planet? Through this corridor thing you were talking about?' Elena blinked rapidly, trying to work out quite how bad this was. She knew that some countries forbade people from bringing in any plants which weren't native, because it could mess up their ecology. 'Are they going to infest our world?'

'Not if I can help it,' said Carra, getting something else out of her bag now—that strange metal pyramid she'd been using last night. 'This is what he's been doing. He has mixed pollen from the harandela plant with an Earth species; most likely a species that is already fast-growing and invasive.'

'Japanese knotweed,' murmured Elena. The stems on those flowers looked very similar to the Japanese knotweed Mum had pointed out to her.

'The harandela is loved on Ayot,' said Carra. 'It is on the planet's flag. But Earth people won't love it. It may be beautiful but it consumes oxygen and converts it to carbon dioxide.'

'Don't some of our plants do that?' Elena asked.

'Yes—at night. Some do it at night. Then they convert the CO_2 back to oxygen in the day. Harandela doesn't convert it back.'

'So . . . you're telling me this flower is sucking up all our oxygen?' Elena felt her breathing constrict just thinking about it.

'Not all. Not yet. But it will.' Carra leant over and flicked something on the cardboard cone. It fizzed and lit up just like the firework it resembled. 'Stand back,' said Carra. She pushed

Elena further back along the gravel path and then pressed the pyramid gadget. Once again Elena heard its whispering buzz and felt the magnetism. Even though they were both outside it this time, she sensed the force field leaping up and covering the entire greenhouse and kitchen garden.

She grabbed Carra by the arm and said: 'Wait! Before you do anything—there are friends of mine in there.' Carra glanced around them. Elena added: 'Nobody's coming. Please . . . Give me sixty seconds!' Carra nodded. She clicked the pyramid again and the force field evaporated.

Elena closed her eyes, let out a long slow breath, and sent the clearest message she could think of: *All of you! It's time to go! Go NOW. Go NOW!* For an agonizing few seconds she thought she had failed; that they hadn't heard her. Then, to her rising relief, first insects and then spiders, then a handful of birds roosting in the blackberry bushes, and finally dozens of mice, voles, rats, and rabbits began to stream out, away from the greenhouse and the kitchen garden. They escaped in a widening ring, shaking the grass and sending a thrum of animal energy through Elena's very bones. She was so pleased she had reached the birds and insects too. It would have been terrible to leave them to their fate, just because Matt and Tima had a stronger connection.

Beside her, Carra let out a grunt of amazement. She turned to stare at Elena, with mounting respect in her dark eyes. 'Night Speaker,' she said. She shook her head and then knelt to touch the pyramid at her feet. The force field burst out again, vibrating through the still, late-morning air and covering the garden and greenhouse once more. Elena could just make out its wide dome shape by the way the pollen, spores, and dust, thrown up by the mass exodus of wildlife, were contained within it, dusting the inside curve.

The cardboard cone was inside the dome too and it continued to flicker and glow brightly at the tip; a small blue sparkler. Elena peered at it. What was it doing? Sending out some kind of gas which would wipe out the dangerous plants and their pollen?

The answer came with a boom. Elena shrieked and stumbled backwards as the dome turned into a massive ball of flame.

CHAPTER 31

The paramedics said he was still alive. They picked him up and put him on a stretcher on wheels and rolled him across the quad to the ambulance.

'You're lucky to get us so fast,' one of them muttered to Miss Lanyard, who had rushed into the music block to give first aid to Mr James as soon as she'd heard. Tima had seized the phone on Mr James' desk, ignoring Lily's screams, and called reception. The school's chief first-aider had been on the scene a minute later, and by then reception had already called for an ambulance.

Miss Lanyard looked shaken as her colleague was bumped up into the vehicle, a plastic oxygen mask on his face. 'What's going on?' she said. 'I heard something on the radio.'

'We don't know for sure, but there seems to be some kind of outbreak,' said the paramedic, leaning in towards the teacher and speaking in a low voice which Tima could, nonetheless, hear. 'Breathing difficulties—especially in the elderly or those with underlying illnesses like asthma or bronchitis,' went on the paramedic, looking not too well herself. She coughed and then shook her head. 'I'm not supposed to say anything about this. I think there's going to be an official press conference at the hospital soon. It'll be on the local radio and TV. I'm not meant to say . . . but they think there's something in the air. Something bad.'

Tima felt chilled. What did Lucky keep saying? *Bad mist.*

'I don't care if it's breaking the rules. *I'm* advising you to keep everyone inside the school, with the windows shut,' went on the paramedic, lifting her chin. 'Email parents and tell them to stay home too, until we know what we're dealing with. The kids should be safe inside.'

Miss Lanyard looked even more shaken. 'But Mr James was inside . . .'

'He was probably infected before he got here,' said the paramedic, shrugging.

Miss Lanyard gulped and nodded. 'I'll tell the head right away . . . and . . . the people that you've been bringing in . . . are they OK? Have they . . . ?'

'Can't tell you any more,' said the paramedic, grimly climbing back into the ambulance. And that told them a lot.

'Miss Lanyard,' said Tima, as the ambulance slowly drove out past the knot of worried staff that had gathered. 'I think I might know what happened.'

'Not now, Tima,' said Miss Lanyard. 'I have to tell the head

what's going on. And I need everybody inside. EVERYBODY—
INSIDE!' She shepherded everyone back into the main building
in a voice that would accept no argument. Tima glanced back
at the music block. Nobody else was in there and the windows,
as far as she could see from here, were all shut. The flowers were
contained. If she was right, that was a good thing. A very good
thing.

She sent out a message. *I'm sorry. I didn't pay attention before.*
I'm so sorry. It's the flowers, isn't it? The pollen off them or something.
That's what's been killing some of you. Am I right?

Several flies, bees, and wasps responded, circling down
towards her and sending her vibrations. *Yes. Bad flowers.* How
long had they been here, though? She hadn't seen them in the
music block before today, and none around the school—and the
disintegrating bee; that was a week ago. Of course the bees and
wasps could fly for miles around . . . maybe these rare orchids
were spread around the town. A buzz in her school pinafore
pocket made her surreptitiously dig out her phone. It was
forbidden even to have it on during school hours, but this was
an emergency. She saw a text from Elena:

**THERE ARE POISON ALIEN PLANTS IN THORNLEIGH! WE HAVE
TO FIND MORTO AND STOP HIM!**

Yup. It was all making a horrible sense now.

'Lily!' Tima ran after her singing partner, who was still
weeping hysterically as she walked back into the school
reception. A teacher had been attending to her but that teacher

had now run after Miss Lanyard for more information. 'Lily!' Tima tapped the girl's shaking shoulder. 'Stop crying! Tell me about the flowers.'

'What?' sobbed Lily. 'What are you *talking* about?! Our music teacher is *dying* and you want to talk about *flowers*? You're *such* a freak, Tima Bahar!'

Amid the growing babble in the school's reception area, Tima grabbed both Lily's arms, spun her around and hissed, 'SHUT UP! And *listen*. Those flowers. They are toxic. I think they made Mr James ill. And if *your mum* brought them in . . .'

Lily's mouth dropped open and her eyes grew wide and scared.

'Where did she get them? Has she got some at home?'

'I told you. From Mr Rosen—the head teacher at Harcourt High,' said Lily, her voice now a thin whisper.

'And have you got any at home?'

Lily nodded, looking terrified.

'You've got to call your mum,' said Tima. 'Right now.'

Over by reception, the teachers were all talking urgently about a total school lockdown.

'What's your address?' asked Tima, a sudden realization hitting her with a thump in the chest.

'The Lodge, Stretton Park Lane,' murmured Lily.

Someone hit an alarm button. A high-pitched horn in three, deafening blasts, began to sound every few seconds. In between the blasts a calm automated voice said: *'We are in lockdown. Please remain in your classrooms and close all windows.'* Another three blasts. *'Follow the lockdown protocol. You will be given more information shortly.'*

As teachers scrambled to get back to their classrooms the outer doors began to automatically close.

'Make them call your mum,' yelled Tima, shoving Lily towards reception. 'Tell her to get away from the flowers.'

Lily fled to the receptionists, and Tima stood, thinking furiously about her next move. She'd been in a lockdown drill last term and she knew what was happening. Just behind her the reception doors were slowly closing and seconds away from automatically locking. Tima glanced around again, saw nobody watching, and ran for it.

She sprawled on to the red-tiled step as the doors swung shut behind her and she heard the automatic lock click, sealing everybody in, and sealing *her* out.

She crawled away from the door and around the corner of the building, out of sight behind some shrubs. She could still hear the alarm blasting and the eerie voice delivering its warning inside the school, but nobody was hammering on the reception doors, shouting out after her. They were all too distracted. She'd got away unseen. She was very glad she wasn't in there with them. She just hoped Lily's mum hadn't also delivered some flowers anywhere else inside Prince William Prep. Seemed unlikely. Her classmates and teachers were probably all safe as long as they stayed out of the music block.

And what about her own safety? Tima stood still, calming her breathing. She and Lily had been in the music block for at least half an hour, just around the corner from those plants. But not close enough to inhale the pollen. And . . . hadn't Mr James mentioned he was asthmatic the other day? Like the paramedic had said—he already had a health issue with his lungs.

She had a chilling flashback to the froth coming out of his mouth. That was really scary. She'd never heard of that happening in an asthma attack.

No.

Bad mist.

This was something to do with Carra and this guy Morto. And now there was no more time to lose. She texted Elena:

I KNOW! School in lockdown. I escaped. Where r you?

CHAPTER 32

Without the starlings, he might never have got them an
ambulance. After dialling 999 Matt had been hanging on the
phone, trying to get through, for five minutes. He'd been close to
total panic.

Mum and Dad weren't dead—he knew that much. They
were breathing. He'd wiped away the frothy stuff from their
mouths and put Mum into the recovery position, on her side, on
the floor. Dad, heavier and on the soft mattress, was harder to
move, but he'd managed it, propping him on to his side with a
pillow. Both of them were breathing shallowly, wheezing slightly.
Neither of them responded to his shouts and slaps.

He was on the phone, *willing* somebody to answer, for
minutes on end. This was crazy! Nobody was supposed to *wait*
for the emergency services to pick up. And then he'd heard

sirens. In fact, he realized that he'd been hearing *a lot* of sirens while he semi-slept. Looking outside he saw an ambulance, blue lights flashing, turning the corner of his road. He *needed* that ambulance! NOW!

Matt knew he could never run downstairs in time to stop it. Lucky knew this too. A second later a vast cloud of starlings descended from the sky and swooped low to the road. The ambulance braked. The murmuration hung in front of it like a smoky, shifting entity as Matt stumbled down the stairs, barefoot, across the car-wash forecourt and out into the road. One of the paramedics had climbed out of the passenger seat and was on the road, gaping up at the birds.

'What the hell . . . ?' she said.

'Help!' yelled Matt. 'Please! My mum and dad . . . they're sick . . . they're . . . I think they're dying.'

The paramedic dragged her eyes away from the thousand or so starlings spiralling across the road and frowned at him. 'Symptoms?' she said.

'Breathing not good . . . frothy stuff coming out of their mouths,' said Matt, hearing panic and tears in his voice.

'Phil—we've got some more!' yelled the paramedic. 'We'll have to fit them in.'

The driver stayed put as cars began to build up behind the stalled ambulance and another paramedic emerged from the back of the vehicle. In seconds they were up in the flat and dealing with Matt's parents. They moved fast. Their strained, tired faces showed no surprise at what they found.

'There's no room for you to ride in with us,' said the male

one—Phil—after they'd loaded up their new patients. Mum had been laid on a bench opposite another guy with an oxygen mask on; Dad was on the floor on top of a blanket. 'We shouldn't even take your Dad but it's looking desperate. I'm sorry—but you're going to have to stay behind and call in to find out what's happening. Unless you can get yourself over to A & E.'

Matt nodded. 'I'll get there.'

'Maybe you shouldn't,' said the woman. 'There's something in the air—we think it's making people ill when they breathe it. Were your parents outside before this happened?' Matt nodded, although only Dad had been out. 'You should probably stay at home,' she went on. 'Keep the windows shut. Put the local radio on and listen for information. Thornleigh's in a really bad way today.' She gave his arm a squeeze. 'I'm sorry, love—but we have to go.'

'We're not going anywhere until this stops!' came the slightly hysterical voice of the driver, up front.

'Oh,' said Matt. 'Sorry.' He waved at the birds and they all rose into the air and dispersed.

The female paramedic gave him a startled glance as she clambered up and knelt next to Dad. She seemed about to say something to Matt but then she just rolled her eyes, shook her head, and yelled: 'GO! GO!' to the driver as she pulled the rear doors closed. The sirens shrieked and the ambulance was gone in seconds.

Matt sank on to the wall beside the car wash, shaking. Had he just saved Mum and Dad? Had he done the right thing? And what was going *on*? Should he go back inside and lock the doors and windows? He walked in a daze back to the front door and the stairs up to the flat. But as he reached it Lucky flew across it and seemed to hover, flapping her wings agitatedly at him.

'Bad mist!' she squawked. *'Bad mist!'*

'I know. I have to go in,' he muttered.

'Know!' she replied. Although, he now realized she wasn't repeating his *know*; she was telling him *NO*.

He stopped on the step and held out his fist for her to land on. 'Lucky . . . are you telling me the bad mist is IN there?'

'IN there,' echoed Lucky. Then she sent him an image. It scattered across his mind. Golden dust . . .

Matt rubbed his hands across his crumpled face as it began to make sense. The flowers . . . the *pollen* spilt everywhere. He suddenly thought of Mr Rosen's dead fish. His wheezing cough . . . it was the *flowers*. There was something badly wrong with those flowers. Did anybody else know this? Did Mr Janssen know it? Could he have grown something poisonous and not known about it?

'Lucky,' said Matt. 'Is it the flowers?'

'The flowers,' said Lucky. 'Bad mist.'

Matt looked at his bare feet. He was wearing a T-shirt and some pyjama shorts. His clothes and his shoes and his phone were indoors. 'Lucky,' he said. 'I'm going to hold my breath—get in there for my stuff—and come out again. OK?'

'OK,' said Lucky.

Matt took several deep breaths and then ran up upstairs, holding the safe air in his lungs. He hurtled into his room, grabbed his jeans, socks, trainers and a zip-up hoodie, and then hooked up his mobile from the end of the bed. He ran back down the stairs, pausing long enough to grab the door key from its hook, and then burst back out on to the forecourt again, air exploding from his lungs, slamming the door shut behind him.

Out on the concrete he threw on the clothes and trainers and then went to call Elena on his phone. Two messages were waiting on it—one from Elena, one from Tima. He opened Elena's first and saw it was to both him *and* Tima. It read:

THERE ARE POISON ALIEN PLANTS IN THORNLEIGH! WE HAVE TO FIND MORTO AND STOP HIM!

Tima's reply was also to them both and read:

I KNOW! School in lockdown! I escaped. Where r you?

Whatever was going on, it must be all over the town. Certainly sounded like it if the chorus of sirens was anything to go by.

With trembling thumbs he texted back:

Mum and Dad sick. On way to hosp. I'm on my own. Flowers in the flat!

Tima texted a reply almost at once.

They're at my school in music room. Music teacher sick!

Elena pinged back:

**MR JANSSEN was growing them, Matt! He IS Morto! Harcourt
High now in lockdown. Carra blew up greenhouse. Need you
both NOW! Meet at bandstand. RUN! WORSE STUFF TO TELL
YOU!**

Matt glanced around the forecourt. His eye fell upon a very
nice Land Rover Discovery, beautifully clean and spruced. He
ran across to it, flung open the door, and flipped down the sun
visor. Yup. Key right there.

He texted:

On my way.

CHAPTER 33

'Harcourt School, Prince William Prep, your house, Matt, and . . . where did you say, Tima?'

Tima leant on Elena's shoulder, peering at the map, spread out on the wooden floor of the bandstand. 'The Lodge, Stretton Park Lane—that's Lily Fry's house. She said her mum had some at home too.'

Elena marked all the locations on her map in red felt-tip pen, taking a long slow breath to keep her heart from racing. It hadn't really settled down since they'd sprinted away from her school. Within thirty seconds of the greenhouse explosion the alarms had sounded in the main building, shrieking in her ears as she and Carra skidded out through the gates. She knew the school would have gone into lockdown because she'd done the drills . . . Unlike the fire drill, when something happened outside or near the school the students were locked *inside* for safety. She'd heard the eerie piping lockdown horn sounding out as they ran up the road.

Shaking the memory of it out of her head, she tapped the red dots on the map. 'These places are all within a radius of about five kilometres.'

'How long have these plants been *out*?' asked Tima. 'They could be anywhere . . . everywhere! There could be pollen floating all over Thornleigh. We can't track them *all* down and burn them up, can we?' She looked at Carra, who was sitting with them, studying the map with an unreadable expression on her face.

'No. It's not practical to do that,' she said. 'And the pollen isn't the problem.'

'It looked like a problem to *me*!' muttered Matt, sitting on the balustrade of the bandstand. 'My parents are both . . . I mean, they could be . . .' His voice faltered and he shut his mouth in a thin line and glared angrily away from them all. 'I shouldn't be here. I should be at the hospital.'

'No,' said Elena. 'You need to be here. With us.'

'*I* took poisonous flowers *home*!' Matt screwed up his eyes and bunched his fists into his hair. 'I poisoned them.'

'Mr Janssen poisoned them,' said Elena. 'You didn't know.'

'The pollen is not good,' conceded Carra. 'It will blight other plants and kill some of your insects . . . and it causes an allergic reaction in some people. It can make the lungs produce too much mucus. That's what the frothy stuff is. Some people die . . . but some do not die,' she added, giving Matt a kinder look.

'But the pollen is not the *problem* . . .?' Elena prompted, taking another slow breath, wondering if this really could be *real*; some kind of horror epidemic, right here in Thornleigh. The ambulance sirens were still carolling around the town in a chorus of growing panic.

'Thornleigh lies in a deep valley and the air in the town pools there, like stagnant water,' explained Carra, as if she was a science teacher. 'So if it's polluted or . . . changed . . . it can sit here and not be freshened up for days, especially during calm, still weather. It's been calm for days. Morto must have been breeding his hybrid for some weeks—it would have taken that long for him to cross-pollinate the harandela with the knotweed and grow the new species in Earth soil. As the plants reach maturity, three things happen. Stage one: they produce the pollen, which can travel on insects or just on the breeze. That's bad news for the allergic people . . . and some allergic insects or animals . . .'

'I saw what it did,' said Tima, her head drooping. 'It killed a bee . . . and disintegrated it!'

Matt glanced at Tima, gulping. Elena put a hand on his shoulder and squeezed.

'Stage two,' went on Carra, still in Science Teacher Mode, 'it starts to draw in oxygen and put out carbon dioxide in its place. Just one plant can draw in a tremendous amount of gas. Over a few days this will thin the atmosphere nearby and also affect anyone with lung conditions or other health issues. Even fit people will start to feel it, especially at night when there's naturally less oxygen anyway.' She looked at the gadget on her wrist, tapped it and lifted her finger. A holographic column rose up, showing some figures. 'Over the past week the oxygen levels in Thornleigh have dropped from 20.9 per cent to 19.5 per cent. This is only just enough for you to be able to breathe. And closer to the harandelas it drops to around sixteen per cent.'

Elena felt her own breathing tighten. 'Why would he do this? Mr Janssen . . . or, I mean, your Morto guy . . . ? What does he want?'

Carra blinked at her. 'He's not *my* Morto,' she said. 'And what do you *think* he wants?'

'Oh come *on*!' Matt stood up, bouncing on the balls of his feet and shoving his fists deep into his hoodie pockets. 'You're not saying he wants to take over the world!'

Carra stood up too. '*He* might not, but the people he works for do. Ayot has terraformed a planet before. They know how to do it. Introduce an Ayotian plant which can be hybridized with a native species, then just let it grow. Harandelas grow *fast*. They could cover your whole country in three weeks.'

'And it's *out*—escaped! All around us already?' Elena felt panic rising through her chest. 'We're too late!'

'No,' said Carra. 'It hasn't got to stage three.'

'But . . . the pollen . . .' whimpered Elena, waving all around her as if the alien pollen was showering from the skies.

'. . . has nowhere to go and nothing to pollinate,' said Carra. 'Not yet. The plants he has produced cannot pollinate each other. The next generation will. But the seed pods haven't triggered yet. That will be stage three.'

'Seed pods?' asked Tima.

Carra pulled a notebook and pencil from her backpack and sketched something they'd all just got very familiar with. The harandela plant was tall and graceful, with its beautiful petals and curling stamen. She sketched the round blobs on its straight, bamboo-like stems; with a star shape across them, these looked a bit like small sea urchins clinging on to the plant. 'These are the seed pods,' she said. 'They all go off at the same time. They *explode* and send seeds into the air. They wait for their moment. It's always at night and it's always in high wind. Something in each plant detects the dropping of air pressure when high winds are coming—it knows just when to go. Now . . . once the seeds are out and the new plants are growing as fully developed hybrids, right from seed, *then* the pollen will have somewhere to go. But that won't matter to you, when it happens.'

'Why?' asked Tima.

'Because you'll all be dead.'

There was a moment of complete silence. Even the distant sirens seemed to stop for a few moments.

'Dead?' whispered Tima, at last, her dark eyes huge and fearful.

'Yes,' said Carra. 'If we don't stop Morto before the seeds blow out, they will travel around your planet in a matter of hours. The plant will seed itself in the soil, then it will cross-pollinate and grow out of control in a just a few weeks. And as it grows it will take your oxygen faster than your native trees and marine algae can replace it. You will all suffocate. Before Christmas, probably.'

Elena could hear her heartbeat pulsing through her ears.

Not for the first time, her brain was doing all it could to reject what it was hearing, flinging itself this way and that like a panicked cat. *It's a dream. A dream. Not real.*

'An advance party of Ayotian colonists will probably be here by New Year, when the new atmosphere is stable,' went on Carra. 'They'll vaporize all the human and animal remains and bring some of their own planet's species to get settled in. About a year from now, this will look more like Ayot than Earth.'

She glanced around at them all. 'In case you were wondering, that's why we need to find Morto.'

CHAPTER 34

As he washed the dried blood out from under his black fingernails, Spin experienced something unusual.

A pang of regret.

It was such a rare feeling that for some seconds he really didn't know what it was. Something in his chest felt . . . compressed. And it wasn't just the touch of bronchitis he seemed to have been battling for the past week. No. It was an *emotional* weight, and he felt it at the very moment he thought back to last night in the Night Speakers' den.

Emotion wasn't his thing. If he was going to be honest with himself, though, he had to admit it was *pure* emotion which had driven him to snag Car-wash Boy up in the branches and give him a little bit of fang action. Matt had made him *rage*. His sneery, dismissive words; '*He thinks he's a vampire!*' It had needled something deep inside—with dramatic consequences. One second he was having a genuinely interesting conversation with (apparently) an alien—the next, he'd gone feral and vampired the Prince of Squeegees into silence.

It had been *very* satisfying to see the shocked look on his upended face and there was no doubt he deserved it. But . . . Spin winced, smiling tightly over his gritted teeth as he acknowledged it to himself . . . he had *not* enjoyed the look on Elena's face. In the split-second before he'd pulled off his smoky exit, he'd seen her expression. Horror and dismay.

Just a few weeks ago he would have been very happy with a horror and dismay score like that. Cute girls freaking out was really a big part of the game—but that was when a cute girl was only that: a two-dimensional extra in his self-directed movie. Hey, *you*! Look cute and scream! *Aaaand—action!*

It was all good until you found out the cute girl was an actual *person* with a backstory.

Spin knew things about Elena. She was brave and stubborn. She was clever and good and cared a lot about other people. She played the cornet quite well. And . . . she was vulnerable. Now, she was horrified too. At him. She was never inviting him in for tea now.

Good thing too, he told himself. *She's not part of your world. She might be out in it, but that's not the same. She's not like you. She's way too sweet.*

He lay back on his bed and stared up. There were stars above him, glowing like the real thing. He knew all the constellations and had spent many hours painting a replica of them on his midnight-blue ceiling, using glow-in-the-dark paint. He liked to wander across his sky, reciting all the stars, moons, and nebulae to himself; it helped him sleep in the bad times. Right now, though, it was hard to concentrate. What *was* going on in Thornleigh today? It sounded like downtown New York; he'd never heard so many sirens.

With a sigh of exasperation he flung himself back on his feet and went to the window. Positioning himself at a well-practised angle, flat against the wall, he twitched open the thick black curtain. A dagger of daylight shot through, despite the black gauze net across the glass, but he was safe in shadow. Through the gauze he could see directly on to street level; his eyes resting on the heels and wheels of the people of Thornleigh as they went about their daily business. Some heels went by fast; running. Some dragged and stumbled. Someone shouted. Another siren sounded. A white van pulled up, its engine rattling unheathily. It gave off a sudden, expensive-sounding BANG, and died right in front of his basement window, efficiently blocking his view.

Spin sighed, let the curtain drop safely back, and then unearthed his old-fashioned analogue radio from under the bed, pulling out its aerial. When he'd found the local BBC station he learnt that Thornleigh *was* in crisis. The usual afternoon show had been dumped and there was live rolling news from two or three reporters—all of them staking out parts of Thornleigh. One was hyperventilating her report from outside the hospital; one was stopping people in the town centre and demanding to know if they were breathing OK (many not, apparently)—and another was at the town hall, ready for some kind of statement to be announced by the leader of the council.

'If you've just tuned in,' said the presenter, 'we're about to hear from the council leader of Thornleigh regarding an emergency situation. I must stress that we have no confirmation of what's happening just yet, but what we *do* know, thanks to calls from BBC Radio Suffolk listeners, and also to our team of reporters in Thornleigh right now, is that there seems to be some kind of air pollution crisis. Thornleigh A & E is handling multiple casualties, all experiencing breathing difficulties. Again, it's not yet official, but we are recommending everybody should stay inside and keep doors and windows shut.'

Spin sat back on the end of his bed and pressed his hand to his chest. A whole *new* emotion started running across this skin. This was clearly a day for fresh experiences. He was feeling . . . *fear.* Not much. Just a little, prickling below the surface of his natural cool. Bronchitis. That's what he'd thought he had. A little inflammation—a mild virus probably. Nothing that could affect *him.*

But no. Something else. Toxic *air?*

Come *on.* It couldn't be *that* bad, could it? Nobody was dropping in the street. It was most likely the power station, leaking gas. They'd mended the stack on it pretty fast after the fire back in the summer. They'd probably done a rush job and now it was sending out fumes at ground level. It would all be sorted by tonight and he could get out and track down Elena and the others and find out what Waspy Wendy had told them about this intergalactic baddie she was after.

He heard someone muttering and realized whoever it was had sat down very close to his window. He pulled the curtain back again, carefully, to listen in. Someone was having a phone conversation.

'I have broken down,' the guy said, and went on to give his location in a precise, slightly accented voice. 'I need to have my van mended. Can you send me a mechanic with a replacement cambelt, please? I know. I heard. People are panicking over nothing. Can *you* breathe? Good. So can I. Please send your mechanic. I will pay three times what you would usually ask. Yes. No. I will wait here.'

Spin peered up through the black gauze and saw the van driver's left knee and elbow as he sat down against the wall of the building, oblivious to an observer in a basement, thirty centimetres away from him. The man began to hum a little song. Occasionally he laughed to himself, as if he had some huge joke running in his head.

Spin went back to bed.

CHAPTER 35

'Our friends,' said Tima. 'They can help us find this Morto guy.' She glanced from Elena to Matt and they nodded back at her.

'We'll ask,' said Elena. She closed her eyes. Matt consulted quietly with Lucky. Tima closed her eyes too and sent out a message to the flying insects. *Here he is . . . see the picture in my head . . . find him. Show us where he is.*

They all felt the response—and even saw and heard it as birds took off in the trees, squirrels leapt across the branches, and flies, beetles, bees, and wasps rose into the air around the bandstand.

Then they felt the drop. The sudden plummet of energy. And saw it too—insects raining down and birds slumping back into the trees, squirrels sliding down the bark, scrabbling weakly for a claw-hold.

'The animals,' said Elena, her eyes wide and worried. 'They're not feeling so good either.'

'Yes,' said Carra. 'They will be affected too. Some more than others.'

'STOP!' Tima said. 'Only help if you're fit and well.'

Elena and Matt repeated this, instinctively saying it aloud as well as sending it from the Night Speaker part of their minds. Matt held on to Lucky. 'No,' he said. 'You stay with me. The others can look. You stay with me.' He clutched the bird close to his chest, tucking her rainbow black head under his chin like a protective dad.

'They're still helping,' said Tima to Carra. 'But I don't know how long it will take. They're weak—and if we push them . . . they won't survive this. I've asked the cockroaches. They can manage. They could withstand a nuclear blast. And they can go on for days without a head . . .'

'OK—we need a plan!' Elena stood up straight and glanced around at them all. Tima could see her friend was scared—as scared as *she* was—but she was getting a hold of herself. That made Tima stand up too. 'We can't just sit here, waiting to hear back from cockroaches. We have to make a plan.'

'Yes,' agreed Tima. 'Let's go back to my place. We can have a hot drink and . . . check out the weather and stuff.'

Matt peered at her, looking baffled.

'Because of what Carra said,' explained Tima. 'About the seeds . . . waiting for the wind.' But mostly she just wanted to be somewhere that felt safe. Even if it wasn't.

'Yes,' said Carra, smiling as if she understood. 'Let's do that.'

'But what about your mum and dad?' asked Matt. Tima had never brought Matt back to her house. Elena had visited a couple of times, but her friendship with a fifteen-year-old boy was a bit harder to explain—especially when she had only just turned eleven and the boy wasn't even in her school.

'Mum and Dad are at work,' said Tima. 'My school will probably have texted them about the lockdown; they'll think I'm safely in class.'

'Unless your school has worked out you've gone AWOL,' said Matt. 'They've probably noticed by now.'

Tima shrugged. 'Maybe—but I haven't had a call or a text yet. They don't always pick up messages quickly. Dad might be in theatre and Mum could be out on a farm somwhere. Come on. Let's go back. We need something to eat and drink too.'

Matt looked ill-at-ease as she let them into the black and white tiled hallway. She led them all straight through to the kitchen and flicked on the plasma screen on the wall, finding the twenty-four-hour news station. Then she got the kettle and said: 'Tea, coffee . . . ?' just the way Mum did whenever visitors dropped by.

Carra settled on to a high stool, resting her elbows on the granite-topped island unit. 'More cocoa, perhaps?' she said, her eyes fixed on the screen. The weather report hadn't come on yet but it would soon, Tima knew. Elena and Matt wanted cocoa too, so she got milk out of the fridge, hot-chocolate powder from the cupboard, and got on with making it. *There's an alien in your town, planning to destroy mankind,* mentioned a voice in her head, *and you're making cocoa . . . ?*

'Look!' said Elena. 'We're on the crawler!'

Tima turned around to watch a strip of words scrolling across the bottom of the screen, below the network presenter who was interviewing a politician about some issues in Parliament. The crawler read: . . . *alert in Thornleigh, Suffolk, after hundreds of residents hospitalized with breathing difficulties. Local people told to stay indoors with windows shut. Emergency services stretched . . . New baby for reality TV star Jazmeena . . .*

'That's it then,' she sighed. 'The end of the world is coming and it gets three sentences on News 24.'

'They don't know it's coming,' murmured Elena.

'Is there any chance this Morto guy is still at your school?' asked Tima.

'No,' said Elena. 'Carra has this bio-reading gadget. She used it just outside the gates, while the kitchen garden was on fire and the school was going into lockdown. We did think he might be inside but her bio thing showed he'd left the building, probably in his car or van, about ten minutes before we first got there.'

'Couldn't you just follow the trace?' asked Tima.

'It's short range,' explained Carra, 'Just 200 metres. And I don't think he will go back to the school—not when he sees the smoke from the garden. He'll know. He'll know I'm coming for him.'

'So—we've got his picture,' said Tima. 'Why don't we send it to the police—get them to hunt for him? We could do it anonymously; tell them he's a terrorist or something. Say he's letting off toxic gas in Thornleigh.'

'No,' said Carra. 'It must be me. He has alien weapons they

won't recognize. If your police approach him there will be many dead. I have better weapons. We just have to find him. Soon.'

Just *how* soon became clear at that moment. The weather forecast was on. The map showed a huge LOW creeping across England, heading from west to east. White arrows swooped in a curve right across East Anglia. 'High winds, up to gale-force eight, should reach the eastern part of the country around midnight, peaking to gusts of force nine,' explained the pretty, dark-haired weather presenter. 'There may be some disruption, especially in coastal parts, so a Met Office amber weather warning is in place.'

Carra stared down at the gadget on her wrist. It looked a bit like the watch Tima's dad had which connected with his smartphone and laptop. But it was hexagonal in shape and, once again, she was pulling holographs out of it under her fingertips; they looked like swirling weather fronts. 'I concur,' she said.

'You've got a weather app on your watch?' demanded Matt. 'Why didn't you just tell us?!'

'I wanted to see if it agreed with your Met Office people,' explained Carra. 'It does. Wherever Morto is now, tonight he will be somewhere high. At . . .' she consulted her wrist again. '. . . two in the morning, I predict, he will be in a high place with as many harandela plants as he can get there. Where is a high place?' She pinged her wrist gadget with her knuckle. 'My geo-mapping is not good enough. It glitches.' She huffed at it. 'It was perfect before I came here.'

'Well, that's what shooting through an interdimensional corridor will do for you,' said Elena, trying to smile. 'Fries your wiring. I'm not sure about the highest point . . . Leigh Hill probably, over the old quarry. Or maybe St Catherine's Mount . . . over the eastern side.'

'So we've got some time,' said Tima. 'Not much—but *some*. Do you think he might release the seeds sooner?'

'He can't,' said Carra. 'The plants decide when. They can sense the low air pressure building. They instinctively know when the best moment to release has arrived. All Morto can to do is watch the weather and then get them in the best position; in a high place. So yes, we have some hours yet to find him.'

'And some hours to find the other flowers and torch them,' said Tima. 'OK—so we know where at least three batches are. In my school music block, at Lily Fry's mum's place and at your school, in the head's office.'

'There were loads,' said Matt. 'He kept them near his aquarium. His fish all died,' he added. 'And there's the one at my place.'

'So . . . we have to get to these places and torch the flowers,' agreed Elena. 'At least stop them causing any more bad reactions like with your mum and dad, Matt.'

Matt nodded, gulping. He'd been on his phone several times now, trying to get through to the A & E department at Thornleigh Hospital, but it just kept ringing. 'Look—if we've got some time,' he said, 'I need to go to the hospital now. Find out what's happening with them.'

'OK . . . here's the plan then,' went on Elena. 'Matt goes to the hospital—finds out how his parents are —and also spreads the word about the flowers. If you can find a reporter and tell them, Matt, that would be good. I bet there'll be loads there.'

Matt nodded. He drank down a little of the cocoa Tima had put in front of him and then headed for the door, Lucky on his shoulder, the Land Rover keys in his hand.

'Matt—it'll be better to run,' said Elena. 'You can cut across the rec and the woods just as fast . . .'

'But—' Matt began.

'There are loads of police around,' Elena cut in. 'You don't want to get caught driving and get yourself arrested.'

Matt sighed, dumped the keys back on the kitchen table, then stalked off towards the hallway.

'Whatever happens,' Elena called after him. 'Stay in touch.'

'I will,' said Matt.

'I will,' echoed Lucky. The door thudded shut and they were gone.

Tima and Elena glanced at each other and then at Carra.

'Can we go and torch some flowers now?' asked Tima.

Carra drained her cocoa, put the mug down with a clunk, and stood up. 'Yes,' she said. 'Let's go.'

Elena held up her hand. 'Before we do . . . should we get online and put a warning out on social media? Tell people to stay away from the flowers . . .'

Carra shrugged. 'If you think it will help,' she said.

'Don't you?' asked Elena, as Tima opened the family laptop.

'Sure. Why not?' said Carra.

Tima couldn't explain why Carra's response gave her a dull chill.

CHAPTER 36

Matt saw the reporters in the hospital car park, some with microphones and recording gadgets, some with a cameraman in tow. There was a network TV satellite truck and a local radio car, with its mast extended high into the air.

It was a news journalist's dream: ambulances screaming in and out, unloading fresh victims; the public, some wearing face masks, looking terrified, some sobbing their fears into microphones. A hospital spokesperson arrived to make a statement in front of the cameras just as Matt got there, Lucky flying above him and perching on the canopy over the main entrance.

'Ladies and gentlemen,' began the spokesperson, a balding man looking sweaty and stressed in a suit. 'Here is what we know. Since 7 a.m. this morning we've admitted one hundred and nineteen patients experiencing breathing difficulties. We're getting many more calls as I speak—for the same symptoms—and doing everything we can to get paramedics out to them as soon as possible. Hospitals across East Anglia have been sending extra ambulance crew to support us.'

'Has anyone died?!' yelled one of the reporters.

The man took a deep breath, glanced down at his notes, and replied: 'So far, we have, sadly, had seven deaths.'

There was a stunned silence, followed by a rush of reaction from the crowd. Matt reacted too. His heart seemed to stand still in his chest. Were his mum or dad among that seven?

'These were all people with underlying health conditions,' went on the spokesperson. 'Their families are being informed. The rest are being treated and many are responding well.'

'What's causing it?' yelled another reporter.

'We don't know,' went on the spokesperson. 'The local authority is urgently investigating—and a specialist team is on its way from London. The advice is to go home and keep your doors and windows shut.' He coughed as if to underline his point.

Matt felt the lull and, encouraged by Lucky watching him from above, he shouted out: 'IT'S PLANTS! We have an ALIEN PLANT in Thornleigh!' The cameras swivelled towards him and he realized that most of the reporters were staring at him like he was a nutter, but he had to seize his moment. This was probably on live TV. He shouted again: 'If you see any big, tall, orchid-like plants—with round seed pods on their stems—GET AWAY! Don't breathe in the pollen!'

The cameras were converging on him now. 'Where have you heard this?' asked a young woman, stepping towards him with a bright-red microphone held out.

'I saw it,' gulped Matt. 'My mum and dad are in there.' He nodded towards the hospital. 'I found them—unconscious. There was pollen everywhere,' he added. It wasn't strictly true but he needed to get the message across. 'From a weird orchid I brought home from school. Just . . . tell everyone . . . stay away from orchids!'

The news people started to push even closer at this point, but Matt ducked down into the crowd behind him and fled into the hospital. There was a huge mob at reception. It would take for ever to get news about his parents if he queued politely. *Lucky*, he called. *I need you.*

A moment later his friend flitted in through the main entrance and glided along, just beneath the ceiling, to land on his shoulder. Such was the cacophony and panic all around him, nobody noticed.

Where's Mum and Dad? sent Matt. *Can you find them?* Lucky flew off down a corridor. One or two people gave her a startled glance, but were too distracted to react any further. At the end of the corridor he saw her fly left and then, a few moments later, return and go right. Twenty seconds later she was back. He walked down the route she'd shown him, turning right, pushing past hurrying nurses and doctors and heading for a double door, jammed halfway open, which had a big red 'NO PUBLIC ADMITTANCE' sign on it. Matt ignored the sign and walked through into an emergency room *packed* with sick people, lying on beds and trolleys . . . a couple even stretched out on blankets on the floor. Beeping equipment punctuated the shouts and grunts of the medical staff intent on saving lives. Most of the patients had oxygen masks on. Some were moving, some were still. One large figure, on a trolley close to him, was covered completely with a blanket. Matt's heart dropped. What if that was Dad? No. No. It couldn't be. Lucky would know.

With Lucky now on his fist, tucked just inside his fleece, he walked on through the room. Nobody stopped him. Towards the back he saw patients who seemed to be in a calmer state. Fewer staff moved among them and at the far end, some were being wheeled through another set of double doors. It was here that he found his mum. She lay, propped up, with an oxygen mask on. Matt ran to her, grabbing her fingers with his free hand. She opened her eyes and smiled weakly at him.

'Mum!' It came out as a sob. 'Are you OK? Where's Dad?'

She squeezed his hand and, muffled under the mask, she said: 'We're OK. Dad's been taken up to the ward. We're OK.'

A nurse came up. 'What are you doing in here?' he demanded. 'No family allowed in here! It's a quarantine zone!'

Matt kissed Mum on the cheek and ran for it. Lucky still under his fleece, he sprinted through the hospital and slid out through the main entrance without bumping into any more reporters. His heart was pounding but full of relief. They were OK. They were *OK*.

Out on the main road he sank on to a concrete wall near a bus stop, letting Lucky flutter up above him and roost in a tree. He got out his phone and sent Elena and Tima a text.

Mum and Dad OK. I warned about orchids on live telly.

A minute later a text pinged back from Tima.

Brilliant! Meet us at your school in half an hour!

A bus rolled up at that moment; one that would take him close to Harcourt High. Matt called Lucky back under his fleece and got on it. The driver had a white cotton mask on. He took Matt's money and mumbled through it: 'I hope you're heading home, son. This is my last journey today. The buses are all finishing their routes and heading back to the depot.'

Matt nodded. 'Good,' he said. Six nervous-looking passengers stared at him as he made his way to the back seat. Four had masks on and the other two were holding handkerchiefs to their faces. Should he do the same? *Lucky*, he sent. *If you start to feel bad . . . just peck me, yeah?*

But Lucky seemed to be OK. He wondered if keeping still and calm kept you safer. You didn't breathe in so quickly when you were still and calm, did you? The birds roosting quietly in the trees would probably be OK. It was just those out flying who might suffer. Back at the bandstand he'd called them all back and stopped them putting themselves at risk . . . but if they hadn't found this Morto guy by this evening, what then? Would he be asking his avian friends to risk everything?

He might not have a choice.

Matt concentrated on keeping still and calm. Lucky seemed to do the same, nestled against his chest. At the stop near the school, Matt jumped off. 'Stay away from big orchids,' he muttered to everyone as he left. They stared back at him across their masks and didn't reply.

The streets were empty. A few people looked out from closed windows but he couldn't see anybody else outside as he made his way down Weybrook Road, past eerily quiet council blocks and shuttered shops. Even the sirens seemed to have quietened down. Lucky broke out from his fleece and flew above him. She seemed OK, so far.

And there was *one* person up ahead. A boy about his age, running, hood up. Probably freaked out, trying to get home. Matt kept his own head down. Which was why he didn't see it coming.

Five seconds later he was smashed into a hedge and dropped to the ground with a vicious kick to the chest. Another kick to the head was all it took to knock him out cold.

CHAPTER 37

Carra had decided she could drive the Land Rover. She studied the manual in its glovebox with great intensity for about five minutes. Then she said: 'Right.' And got behind the wheel.

The journey was slightly worse than their travels with Matt. Carra might be an interdimensional space traveller but she didn't have much instinct for a manual gearbox and they had to yell at her to stop at red lights. But she still managed to get them to Tima's school without crashing, pulling over twice to allow an ambulance past on the way. The music block was right on the perimeter of Prince William Prep; its high windows overlooking the road. One was ajar.

Carra ran at the wall and scaled it in seconds, hauling herself up on to the sill. Then she pushed the window open and climbed through, leaving Tima and Elena on the pavement, staring up anxiously. Three minutes later she was back, landing lightly next to them and leaping back into the driver's seat.

'All done?' asked Tima.

'All done,' confirmed Carra. 'Ashes.'

Her driving improved as bit as they raced to Lily Fry's house.

It was posher than Tima's. The sweeping, herringbone-brick driveway had no cars on it. It looked like nobody was home.

They rang the bell, just to be sure. Tima wondered what on earth they would say if somebody *did* come to the door. *'Um— excuse us. We're just here to torch some of your plants and we'll be on our way!'* But nobody answered.

'How are we going to get in?' asked Elena, peering through the elaborate stained-glass window in the front door.

Tima began to examine the building, looking for open windows. Carra, though, stepped forward with a round black thing in her palm. She pressed it up against the lock on the front door and it clung there like a magnet. Then she pressed a red indent in the centre of the round black thing and there was a series of clicks and the door swung open.

'Wow,' murmured Elena. 'That's handy.'

It felt creepy, walking into Lily's empty house. The hallway was grand, with a huge crystal chandelier hanging over a marble staircase. A massively blown-up photo of Lily, aged about six and looking like a little angel in her ballet tutu, dominated the wall over the turn in the stairs. They tracked through the house, checking in all the rooms for the flowers. They found them on a gold-leafed antique table in a vast sitting room overlooking the garden. The blooms were clustered together, planted in a white ceramic trough. They looked stunning.

And the woman lying on the carpet beneath them looked stunned.

'Oh no!' Tima ran forward. 'It's Lily's mum!'

Elena joined her next to the body. Lily's mother was blonde and perfect like her daughter . . . but her perfection was spoilt by the froth dripping out of her mouth. 'She's still alive,' said Elena, touching Mrs Fry's throat. 'But we have to get her to hospital.'

'It'll take ages—the ambulances are already out for everyone else,' moaned Tima. She felt strangely responsible for Lily's mum, though she didn't know why. 'We should have come here *first*.'

'We'll drive her,' said Carra, decisively. 'Drop her in and then go on to Matt's place and Harcourt High. But first . . .'

She stood up, created a bubble around the harandelas, and then exploded them in a perfectly contained ball of flame. It raged for a few seconds, like a fiery planet, and then, starved of oxygen, the flames subsided. All that was left was a pile of charred twigs and ashes, settling into the trough and drifting on to the antique table.

Tima gaped. 'That's a neat trick.'

But there was no time to marvel at Carra's pyrotechnics. Between them they lifted Lily's pale, wheezing mum, who was surprisingly heavy for such a slim, neat woman, and got her into the back seat of the Land Rover. It took them only a few minutes to reach the hospital; the roads were clear. Most people were obeying the advice to stay indoors. Emergency vehicles tore back and forth, though, and a cluster of blue lights twinkled distantly around the power station. It looked like everyone was focused on that as the possible source of the problem. *Had Matt's claim about the flowers got any more airtime on TV? Had anyone looked into what he'd said or just dismissed it as nonsense?* Tima wondered. *Was Elena's online warning going viral . . . ?*

She patted Mrs Fry's beautifully conditioned hair, wiped some of the froth from her mouth with a tissue, and said, 'Don't worry. We're getting you to hospital. You'll be in the best hands.' She'd heard people say that on TV dramas. It was true. It didn't mean the victim would live, but it was true.

'And Lily's safe,' she added. 'Safe at the school.' Would Lily take good care of *her* mum, if the roles were reversed? She hoped so.

They drove right on to the ambulance drop-off area, even though it wasn't allowed. 'We *are* an ambulance, right now,' Elena pointed out, as they flung open the doors. 'OVER HERE!' she yelled to some paramedics who'd just unloaded another frothing victim. They ran across with a wheeled stretcher and as soon as they had Mrs Fry on board, Elena and Tima jumped back into the car.

'Her name is Mrs Fry!' Tima yelled through the open window as Carra pulled away at speed. 'She got too close to the flowers. Tell everyone to stay away from the FLOWERS! They look like oooooorchiiiids!'

The sky was darkening, with low, grey clouds scudding in from the west as they journeyed on. Tima remembered the weather forecast and gulped as she recalled what the high winds would bring. *Where were her insect messengers? Surely the cockroaches had found Morto by now.*

Carra drove fast, tyres squealing as they rounded corners. 'Slow down a bit,' advised Elena, 'or we might get pulled over by the police. There's a lot of them about.'

'Elena . . . do you think it's difficult for my cockroach friends to find Morto because *I* never met him?' asked Tima. 'I mean . . . the insects found Carra easily but *I* knew what she looked like in the flesh. I'd met her. I've never seen this alien school gardener of yours—maybe just sending them a picture I've been shown isn't good enough.'

'You're probably right,' said Elena. 'I think I need to get my guys back on the case. But it's harder with mammals. If he's gone way up high somewhere, even the squirrels will take a while to find him. There are no trees to leap through on the really big hills around here.'

'What about bats?' suggested Tima. 'They're mammals. And they fly.'

'Tima—you're a genius!' said Elena. 'I'll try them now. Can we stop, Carra? I don't think speeding around in a car helps!'

They pulled up near the recreation ground and woods around the corner from Kowski Kar Kleen, so Elena could connect with any bat colonies roosting in the trees. She got out of the car and wandered across the turf, closing her eyes and letting out a long, slow breath. Thirty seconds later a flicker of black shot past their heads, swung around in the sky, and shot past them again.

Elena held her hand out flat, palm down, fingers wide.

Tima gasped in delight as the pipistrelle bat flew to her friend, connected and swung upside down, on her index finger. It flexed its fine leathery wings and then folded them neatly against its mouse-like body as Elena talked softly to it. 'This is dangerous,' she said. 'We don't know how bad it is yet. But . . . if you can find him . . . we can stop this. And you, your babies, and all the animals will be safe. Do you understand?'

The tiny creature rotated its furry head from side to side and blinked its small, glittering eyes. Then it spread its wings, dropped from her finger, and flew away. They watched it for a few seconds before several more joined it, tiny black arrows shooting across the sky, silhouetted in the sun's fading glow behind the clouds.

Elena smiled. 'They're going to help. They're OK. They're night creatures so they're used to thinner air. I hope they won't be harmed.'

'I don't think you can afford to worry too much about a few bats,' said Carra. 'Considering your entire species is on the brink of extinction.'

'Yeah . . . thanks for that,' said Elena, rubbing her face.

'This burning of harandelas—it's probably pointless,' said Carra. 'Without Morto we have no idea how many more there are.'

'It's not pointless if we save another person from having a bad reaction and dying!' snapped Tima. 'My favourite teacher could be dead for all I know, thanks to that poisonous pollen. So, until we know where to go to find Morto, we might as well keep torching the flowers we *can* find.'

Carra shrugged but she said: 'OK—we'll keep going.' A gust of wind tugged at her shiny black plait and she shook her head. 'We've got a few more hours. That's all.' She coughed and pulled out the metal inhaler Tima had first seen her with a few nights ago.

'Are you OK?' asked Tima. 'Did any pollen get to *you*?'

'I have no problem with the pollen,' said Carra. 'I would have little problem with the changing of your Earth gases, either. Not for a week or so. I'm used to Ayot air. No . . .' She held up the little shiny canister. 'This is to help me breathe *your* air. Earth's atmosphere is challenging for someone like me. I couldn't survive here for more than a few days without this.'

'Wow,' said Tima. 'I never thought about that.' She took a deep breath herself. Her lungs felt a little heavy . . . thick. As if there was a shallow pool of custard at the bottom of them. 'Are *you* OK?' she asked Elena.

Elena nodded and headed back to the car. Tima followed, acutely aware of the air travelling in and out of her. And the fear of what exactly was *in* that air, began to gnaw at her very bones.

CHAPTER 38

Spin woke up with a headache.

An engine was whining outside his window and he realized the broken-down van must be getting attention from the mechanic. Muted discussion filtered through the thick curtains as the engine stopped and then started again. He got up, taking a deep breath, which rattled uneasily down into his lungs and returned with a cough.

He could sense, rather than see, that it was nearly dark outside. Not late—only 5.15 p.m.—but a dark October dusk with plenty of low cloud. Pulling back the curtains confirmed this. Outside, the van was still obscuring his view and a man in blue overalls was working on it by the headlamps of his pick-up truck. Spin could only see him up to his waist but he could hear him talking to the driver who was at the wheel.

'Turn the engine over again,' instructed the mechanic.

The engine fired and then spluttered to a halt.

'Well, mate, your cambelt's fine now, but I reckon you might have a dead battery there. I'll take a look.' The mechanic's thick black boots trudged past and he called across: 'What are you carrying? Smells nice.'

'Just some flowers,' said the driver. 'I grow them.'

'Got an allotment myself,' went on the mechanic, now opening the bonnet. 'I grow all sorts there. Where you taking them—to a market?'

'No,' said the driver. 'These are for another place.'

'Do they need a certain kind of soil?' said the mechanic, making clinking sounds under the bonnet. 'My blue hydrangeas need acid soil. I have to add it in or they go pink.'

'They are mountain-growing plants,' said the driver. 'They like high places. Very high.'

'Try her again, mate,' said the mechanic and this time the engine kicked off and stayed running. 'Haven't I seen you before?' he went on, lifting his voice above the engine noise.

'I don't know,' said the driver.

'Yeah—I have. You do the gardening at Harcourt High, don't you? My daughter goes there.'

'Ah yes. I work there part-time.'

'It's been in lockdown today,' went on the mechanic. 'There was a fire in the school greenhouse . . . and the vegetable plot. Hang on, that would have been *your* bit, wouldn't it? Did you see it? Were you there?'

'No,' said the driver, after a pause. 'I was not.'

'Oh, blimey, mate—sorry to be the messenger! My girl got home at teatime and said the whole kitchen garden went up in a ball of flame! What a day, eh? As if the blinkin' bad air wasn't causing enough drama.'

'The whole kitchen garden?' echoed the driver, his voice cooling.

'Yep. Sorry, mate. I'm surprised the school didn't call you about it. Apparently there was some big explosion. They thought maybe a paraffin heater in the greenhouse had leaked.' The bonnet clunked shut. 'You're all done now. New battery.'

'Did they see anybody?' demanded the driver 'Did they see a woman near the garden?'

'Sorry,' said the mechanic. The chirp drained out of his words. 'I mean—I don't know. They *might* have seen someone running away. Kelsey said there might have been two people running but they don't know if they had anything to to with it. Police are going to look at the security camera tapes—but it's not top of their list today, what with all this bad air stuff going on.'

'Someone running? Was it a female? *Male or female?!*'

'Whoa—steady! Steady! Come *on*—hands off, pal! I told you—I don't know.'

'Call your daughter! Ask her!'

'Oi! That's enough. Cool the hell down, mister. Here's your bill. I can take cash or card.'

There was a cry and then the mechanic was sprawling on the ground, his shocked face suddenly coming into view. The van's engine burst into life.

Spin pulled on his boots, grabbed his coat, and ran upstairs and outside. The mechanic was back on his feet, bawling after the driver of the van, who was executing a fast three-point-turn in the narrow road. Spin leapt across its path, not to stop it but to see the man's face. For a second the driver locked on to him. Pale, chilly-blue eyes set into a handsome, square-jawed face; blond hair. Then Spin leapt again, to avoid getting mown down as the van careered away up the road.

'What the *hell* . . . ?' The mechanic was next to him now, rubbing his elbow and creasing his weather-worn face. 'Did you get his number? Tell me you got his number.'

Spin was unaccustomed to the whole public-spirit thing, but he rattled off the car's registration number, absently. More important things were on his mind.

Carra was seeking a man who was working in a nursery. Not with babies, as it turned out, but with plants. Had he just seen her *Morto*? He needed to find Elena and tell her. He hadn't hung around long enough last night to hear what this threat to mankind actually *was*—or if it was even serious. But he'd certainly picked up the vibe from Waspy Wendy that *she* thought it was Armageddon on steroids.

It was way too early for him to be out, but Spin's blood was up. Pounding and prickling through his veins. There was no way he was getting any more sleep. It was after school—Elena would be home by now. OK. Time to show up and see whether she'd speak to him or slam the door in his face.

'Will you be a witness? You saw what he just did!' the mechanic was wittering on.

'Go home,' advised Spin. 'The end of the world is nigh.'

He sprinted through the streets. There were very few people out. He saw some faces at windows but only two pedestrians.

Three ambulances and two fire engines passed him as he ran. It was eerie. Teatime rush hour and hardly anybody about. The radio and TV news had clearly had a big effect. Ten minutes later he skidded to a halt by the concrete path to Elena's front door and caught his breath. Actually, he chased his breath for some time before he finally got control. *Bad air.* This was for real.

'Are you OK, love?'

Spin stood up, getting a grip. A woman stood in Elena's doorway. She was similar to her daughter—pretty and fair-haired with the same soft blue eyes. He nodded, not trusting himself to speak just yet. And then she said it. She actually *said the words*.

'Would you like to come in?'

CHAPTER 39

Carra's lockbusting gadget worked just as efficiently at Matt's place. She got in, incinerated the single plant, and got back into the car in under two minutes. Then they drove on to Harcourt High. The sprawl of yellow-brick buildings was in darkness apart from some security lighting on the outer walls. Normally at this time—getting on for 6 p.m.—there would still be people about; after-school clubs and a few teachers working late. But nobody was here now. It looked like everyone had gone home to lock themselves indoors.

As Carra efficiently undid all the locks, Elena guessed that quite a few people would have got into their cars and driven away from Thornleigh entirely, earlier in the day when the news first broke and the ambulance sirens got too frequent to ignore. They walked along silent corridors, using their torches to light the way. Along the walls their beams picked out art projects and posters for school events. *Is this all about to end?* a small voice inside her asked. *Was there never any point making those school event plans . . . ?*

They found the head's office filled with harandelas. Through the glass top of the door they could see a shelf full of them, just over his fish tank, like Matt had said. The tank—something Mr Rosen had always prized—was empty. On the floor and the desk were more; pots and pots of the flowers. *The plant sale*, Elena remembered. She'd seen posters around school about a plant sale to raise funds.

'Stand back,' said Carra. She opened the door, did her whole bubble-of-flame thing, and left the office coated in ash just a minute later.

Tima and Elena leant against the far wall of the corridor. 'This is really bad, isn't it?' mumured Tima. 'How many more of those things have already gone home with people?'

'Well, at least the plant sale never happened,' said Elena. 'That's something. But we have no idea how many more he gave away. Mr Rosen gave a load to Lily's mum and . . .' She felt fear twisting through her insides. 'I don't know if we can stop this . . .'

'We can stop this,' said Carra, striding up to her, slinging her bag of gadgets back over her shoulder. 'We just need to find Morto. How are your bats doing?'

Elena closed her eyes. She wasn't getting any kind of vibrations—but she was right inside a brick and concrete building, where few animals would venture. 'Let's go outside,' she said.

'You two go out,' said Carra. 'I might as well sweep the rest of the buildings. I will join you both in ten minutes.'

'We'll go down on to the school field,' said Elena. 'It'll be easier to communicate with the animals down there.'

She led Tima outside and down some steps to the large school playing field. It was properly dark now but she could still make out the ash drifting away from the scorched kitchen garden. She sat down on the grass, under some slender mountain ash trees near the corner of the football pitch. Tima joined her. They both closed their eyes to concentrate. It was easier in the dark. Clearer. Soon there were conversations. Insects hovered around Tima and moved in elegant spirals and swirls. The grass around Elena filled with mice, voles, and rats, while bats descended into the branches of the ash trees and hung there, upended, flexing their wings. One of the rats climbed right on to her lap, its delicate whiskers shining in the security lights that glowed on the side of the building, and its paws gently resting on her arm.

There was talk. It wasn't too good. Those creatures who felt able *had* been searching for Morto. But the results were confused. Some thought he was in the town. Others thought he was in the forest. Others still, thought he was in the hills that surrounded the basin valley where Thornleigh lay.

'They're messed up,' said Tima.

Elena nodded. She was beginning to feel pretty messed up herself.

Carra joined them. 'Any news?'

'No, not really,' sighed Elena. 'They think they're seeing him . . . everywhere.'

Carra nodded, as if she had been expecting this.

'It's because of the bad air,' said Tima. 'They're doing their best.'

'I know they are,' said Carra. 'But it's not just the bad air. Morto will have a baffler running by now. Once he heard the news of the fire here he will have known I am coming for him and he will have gone into baffler mode.'

'Baffler?' echoed Tima.

'A device to scatter his trace in all directions,' said Carra. 'It's designed to baffle even trained tracker animals. The only reliable way to find him is to *see* him—and some bafflers can even throw illusions of their wearer into other locations.'

Elena stood up, sending the friendly bat and the others on their way. *Get under cover*, she told them.

'Carra,' she said. 'What are you planning to do?'

'I'm planning to find Morto,' said Carra.

Elena turned to look at her, eye to eye. Carra's beautiful face was clear of stings now; she had recovered superhumanly fast. It reminded Elena that Carra *wasn't* a human. At least, not an *Earth* human.

'You have a plan,' she said. 'Don't you? A—what do they call it? A *contingency* plan.'

'Oh God,' breathed Tima. She'd worked it out too.

'If we don't find Morto for you,' went on Elena, 'you're going to . . . *do* something.'

Carra nodded. 'Of course I have a plan.' She dropped her eyes to the grass and then glanced towards the pile of ashes on the far side of the school field.

'You're going to turn Thornleigh to ash, aren't you?' said Elena.

Carra shook her head. 'No. I have calculated how far the flowers could have travelled since they reached maturity,' she said. 'If I'm not certain I have contained them all, I won't burn Thornleigh.'

She blinked and looked away.

'I will burn most of England.'

CHAPTER 40

A crumpled, feathery body lay close to his face. Matt's eyes slowly focused and saw one small, still foot. Horror pistoned through his chest and he scrambled up into a sitting position, crying: '*Lucky!*'

Gales of laughter came. Young, high, hard voices, barking out dark amusement. 'Lucky?! He calls it Lucky?'

Matt knew who the laughter came from but for a few seconds he didn't care. The loss of Lucky was tearing at his insides . . . ripping his heart out. Then he realized the dead bird wasn't a starling. It was a pigeon. Relief flooded through him. And then rage. He stared around. He was in a cold, grey place. Some kind of basement. Liam Bassiter was right here with him, along with Ahmed and Tyler. There was blood in his mouth and under his nose and his ribs ached horribly. If he wasn't mistaken, he'd just taken a good kicking.

But the bird was not Lucky.

'Where are your birdy mates now, eh?' Liam moved closer to him, glancing around. 'Can't get through reinforced concrete, can they?'

Matt saw there was blood on Liam's face too. And Ahmed and Tyler's. They were covered in scratches and minor wounds. He realized his feathered friends had probably done all they could to save him. That poor pigeon on the floor had paid heavily. How many more were outside? Was Lucky out there . . . dead? No. No, he didn't sense she was dead.

'Where is this?' he grunted, getting to his feet.

'It's my place,' said Liam, swaggering towards him. There was quite a lot more blood drying into the carvings in his hair. 'Garramer Towers. This is where *I* rule. And *you* stay on your knees.'

He shoved Matt down. Matt went to get back up but then he saw the blade in Liam's fist. 'What the hell . . . ?'

'I am KING here,' went on Liam. 'So you stay on your knees, bird freak.'

Behind him Ahmed said: 'Yeah!' and then went into a coughing fit. He didn't look too good, his usually cream-coloured skin seemed almost yellow in the glow of the strip lighting. Tyler's eyes looked red and sore and his lip was torn at the side. He kept darting nervous glances around him. Matt could hear a whirring, whining sound and realized they were in the basement of the tower block, behind the lift shaft.

'Look—there's serious stuff going on today,' said Matt,

trying to keep his voice neutral—not weak, not challenging. 'Haven't you heard? The bad air?'

'Was pretty bad air when we dragged you in here,' said Liam. 'Thought you'd cacked your pants. Tell us about the bird thing. I want to know how you do it. I want you to show me how.'

'Sure—I'll show you,' said Matt. 'Let's go outside.'

'Nah, nah na-ah!' Liam wagged his blade. 'Do you think I'm stupid?'

Matt didn't answer.

'I want you to show me with this.' Liam stepped back and picked something up. Something draped in a yellow, flowery cloth. He put it down on the floor between them and then he took off the cloth with a small flourish, like a scabby, knife-wielding magician. A birdcage was revealed. Inside was a single, confused-looking budgie.

'Make it do stuff,' said Liam. 'Now.'

CHAPTER 41

'How do you know Elena?' asked Elena's mother.

'Um . . . from school,' lied Spin.

'Do you know where she is?' said the mother, filling the kettle and setting it to boil.

'No. I was hoping you might be able to help me find her,' Spin said. He coughed. Not for effect. He couldn't help it. 'She was after some information . . . for a . . . project. I just found out something she wanted to know about. But I've lost her mobile number. I . . . actually I don't have a mobile phone myself.'

'That's unusual in a boy your age,' said the mother. 'Most boys are never off them.'

'Well—they make my head ache,' he said. Which was true. In any case—who would he ever call?

'Can you let me have her number?' asked Spin, with his warmest, most charming smile.

'Well, I can't just give out my daughter's number to a young man I've never met before,' said the mother, smiling warmly back at him. 'However handsome and charming he is. Drink the tea— it'll settle your coughing down.'

Spin took a sip of something which tasted like stewed nettles, trying not to grimace.

'I know—it's disgusting. Stewed nettles,' said the mother. 'With a bit of eucalyptus. What did you say your name was, again?'

'Spin,' he said.

'The less boring half of Crispin?'

He looked up at her, startled. 'Yes. But that's usually *my* line.'

'Ah,' she said. 'I've heard her talk about you to her little friend, Tima. When she thought I was fast-asleep on the couch. That's the thing with my meds . . . sometimes I *seem* to be conked out, but I'm actually able to hear stuff. I'm not just lying there being Lithium Lil. Elena has this whole life that she thinks I know *nothing* about . . . but I know more than she realizes.'

Spin blinked. It was slightly hard to keep up with this woman. 'So can you call her for me? Tell her . . . tell her I've seen Morto.'

'Morto? Oooh—as in "death"?' The woman looked childishly excited. Actually, a lot like Elena.

'Mort being the French for "dead"?' he said. 'Um—yes. That could be right. Er . . . the phone call . . . to Elena?'

'Oh yes—I've been meaning to call her. She should be home by now,' said the mother. 'School closed hours ago. She's probably gone to the library.'

'You do *know* about the bad air thing, don't you?' Spin asked, setting his hot, compost-heap juice back down on the kitchen table with a shudder.

'Yes,' said the mother, absently, picking up a walkabout landline phone and punching a number into it. 'My neighbour came over and told me. But Ellie's a sensible girl. The library will be a safe place.'

He was no expert in normal mothers, but Spin began to suspect Elena's was really not your standard mum. Most would have been frantic by now. It was early evening and the school would have closed normally by 3 p.m., there were multiple ambulances skidding around the town like blue-lit Scalextric cars—and her daughter wasn't home.

'She's wonderful, you know, my daughter,' went on the mother, pressing the phone to her ear. 'I am a very poor excuse for a mother to *her* but she is a wonderful daughter to *me*.'

'I'm sure she is,' said Spin.

'It's gone to voicemail,' said the mother. 'What should I say? Oh—I remember. Elena? Elena, lovely. Your friend Spin is here and he wants you to know he's seen Morto. Give me a call back when you get this—and mind out for the bad air. Come home soon. Love you . . .'

CHAPTER 42

'I want to go home,' said Tima.

Elena put an arm around her friend's shoulders. Carra stared at them both calmly. She had just announced her intention to incinerate tens of millions of people but had offered up no apology.

'Most of England?' repeated Elena, in a dry whisper.

Carra nodded. 'I know it sounds extreme,' she said.

'You think?!' burst out Tima.

'But it is damage limitation. By sacrificing roughly forty-six million people, I will save roughly seven point four billion people. Do you see?'

'Oh yeah,' said Elena. 'You can't argue with the maths.'

'But that's only if I don't find Morto,' added Carra. 'I will track through the hills until I find him, although he will probably not break cover until late into the night. It's best that you leave it to me now. I will find it easier to focus on my own.'

'Can I go home, then?' asked Tima. 'I want to see my mum and dad. Just in case . . . you know.'

Elena nodded. 'We can drop you off,' she said. 'And . . . I might go home too. Mum might be worried.'

Carra looked from one to the other, gravely. 'Yes,' she said. 'You should go home and be with your loved ones. I will drive you.'

As they drove back through the empty streets Tima called Matt and left him a message. 'Carra's burnt the plants at your school, so don't worry about meeting us there now. We can't find Morto. Call us if you know anything. I hope your mum and dad are OK. We think you should just stay with them. Tell them you love them.' Tima ended the call and they drove on in silence.

One or two helicopters were thudding around the skies of Thornleigh but the sirens and blue lights were distant now. It seemed nearly everyone had either heeded the advice and shut themselves indoors or long-since fled the town in their cars. Maybe there was a perimeter set up, though, stopping people escaping in case they were contagious. Elena felt suddenly very tired and sad. Was this really how it was all going to end for her? For Mum? For Tima and Matt? For the animals they had made their family? What was the point of becoming a Night Speaker if it was just for a few months and then everything—*everything* —just ended?

They dropped Tima off, watched her hurry to her door, saw

the light shine out from the hallway and her mother hug her on the step.

'I will drive up to the hills and search the roads and paths,' said Carra. 'I believe Morto will position himself there in time to catch the wind. But If I haven't found him by 2 a.m.—'

'It's game over,' said Elena, softly. 'How will you do it? With the fire-bubble thing?'

Carra nodded. 'I can make it very large,' she said. 'It will contain the fallout for several days before it loses power and fails. By then there will be no danger in the ash.'

'And what about you?' said Elena.

'I will be ash too,' said Carra.

'You mean . . . you'll die with the rest of us?' Elena turned to stare at Carra as she pulled up outside her house.

Carra nodded. 'I cannot create a bubble across most of England and stand outside it,' she said. 'I won't have time to travel to the edge of it. I will be in the centre of it, as you found me in the woods last night. Contained along with the seeds. And the rest of you.' She turned to face Elena and put a hand on her shoulder. 'If this is how it goes, I am so sorry. We will none of us know much about it.'

They drove on in silence apart from Elena's guidance back to her house. Carra pulled the car up outside and let the engine idle. Her driving had improved dramatically across the past couple of hours. 'Carra . . . why would you do that?' asked Elena. 'Why would you give up your life for an alien planet?'

Carra folded her arms across the top of the steering wheel and rested her chin on them. 'I swore an oath when I became a marshal. We must protect other worlds. At all costs. Otherwise I *could* leave you here now, go back to the cleftonique post, and step home in a matter of seconds.'

Elena waited, watching a sad smile weave across Carra's face. 'What's home like?' she asked.

'Beautiful,' said Carra, her eyes faraway. 'There are mountains of green stone . . . malachite, you call it here. And oceans and rivers, like here on Earth. Forests and ice deserts. Cloud cities and ocean cities. Some of my people live in the mountains, but some are in the ocean cities. I wish I could take you there.'

'But you won't,' murmured Elena. 'You won't go home and save yourself. You won't just step back to your family.'

'No,' said Carra, sitting up and dropping her hands into her lap. 'I would like to see the face of my father again. But not if it meant seeing the disappointment in his eyes when he learnt I had sacrificed an entire planet for the sake of my own future.'

Elena took a long breath, trying not to let tears mess up her words. 'I understand,' she said. 'And . . . on behalf of the rest of planet Earth, if . . . if you have to . . . you know . . . thank you. Nobody will ever know what you did, but . . .' She turned her head away and got out of the car. 'Wait,' she said, wiping her face. 'How will we contact you if we do hear back from the animals?'

Carra handed her a small black stick with a green button on one end. 'Set this off,' she said.

Elena looked at the stick and was about to ask what it was but Carra drove away, leaving her alone on the pavement. She tucked the stick thing—probably some kind of flare—into her backpack and headed for her front door. The light was on in the hallway and in the kitchen. She let herself in quietly and called out: 'Mum?'

Mum was upstairs on her bed. She was fully dressed but had obviously decided to take a nap, one hand clutched the side of her throat. In the light of the bedside lamp she looked pale. Elena stepped across to her, heart thudding. Had Mum breathed in bad air? Or bad pollen? But no. She felt warm and she made a soft murmuring sound in her sleep. Elena felt a wave of pure exhaustion. She dumped her bag, took off her trainers, and climbed on to the bed with Mum. Mum, in her sleep, made space for her and cuddled her in.

Elena lay like a child and closed her eyes.

CHAPTER 43

I'm scared of them.

Matt looked into the budgie's shiny dark eyes. *I know,* he sent. *I'm sorry. Let me help you. When I say fly—fly up to the ceiling and perch on the metal ducting. And stay there. No matter what happens—just stay there. It's not safe for you to go anywhere else.*

'Come on then,' said Liam, giving the cage a kick and sending the bird into a panicked flurry of blue feathers. 'Aunty Lil's going to go crazy when she wakes up and her little Bertie's gone. When she finds out it was me her old man's going to slap me from here to next week so you'd better make it worth my while. Make it do something.'

'Who do you think I am? Derren Brown?' said Matt.

Liam pointed the blade to the scratches and nicks on his

face. 'You did this,' he growled. 'You made the birds do this. Don't think you can fool me. I *know*.'

'Yeah,' said Ahmed and went into another fit of coughing.

Matt sighed and reached for the cage. He opened the door and put his hand inside. Bertie hopped straight on to his fingers, clinging to him like a frightened child. Matt's heart clenched in sympathy. He gently brought the bird out of the cage, stroked its head, and then mumured: 'Now,' into its soft feathers.

The bird immediately flew up and perched on the dusty metal ducting just below the ceiling.

The boys stared up at it and then back at Matt, expectantly. He looked at them, shrugged, and said: 'Fly in a circle!' *Don't*, he told the budgie, using the direct line from his mind. The budgie stayed still. 'Fly to me!' yelled Matt, holding out his left fist and pointing to it. *Just stay put.* The budgie didn't move. 'I *said—FLY TO ME*!' The budgie preened its left wing.

It took about five minutes to thoroughly disappoint Liam. Liam was *so* disappointed he flung Matt up against the wall, pushing the blade at his throat. Matt could hear and *feel* his wheezing breath. 'You're not fooling me,' he said. 'That's a tame one. It's the wild ones you control. I want to see you do it. NOW.' He grabbed Matt and dragged him along the basement corridor and around the corner into the lift. 'You're coming up to my flat and we're going out on the balcony and if you don't make some pretty patterns in the sky for me . . . you're going off it.'

All three manhandled him into the lift: a small metal box covered in graffiti and smelling of stale urine. They punched the button for floor fifteen and the lift began to rise. Ahmed had another coughing fit and Matt took some small comfort in the look of deep unease on his face as he glanced from his former friend to his new one. Had Ahmed worked out yet that Liam was a psycho? That he really *might* throw someone off his balcony? The lift hadn't begun to climb before its doors began to open again. Liam banged on the metal walls and yelled out. 'It's in USE. Wait for the next one!'

In the sliver of view which Matt got as the doors opened and closed all he could see was a riot of colour. Golds, creams, whites, yellows, and pinks. He froze as a clipped voice slipped in past the closing lift doors. 'Go ahead. *I've* got time.'

Matt's heart began to race even faster in his chest. 'That's Mr Janssen,' he said. 'From school.'

'Yeah. So what?' said Tyler. 'He lives here, thicko.'

Matt felt his insides sink as the lift rose again, whistling and whining up through the shaft. 'What floor?' he asked. Although he already knew.

'Top floor—but don't think you can get away and run to *him* for help,' said Liam.

'Didn't occur to me,' grunted Matt.

Liam's flat smelt of cigarettes. Nobody else was home. Liam dragged him past the kitchen, which was filled with empty takeaway boxes, and on through the sitting room, which was filled with *more* empty takeaway boxes and some crushed cans. Double doors opened out on to a balcony with a view across the town of Thornleigh. Liam pulled one open, allowing a cold gust of wind to rattle the boxes and cans, and dragged Matt outside. It was dark now and the town glittered below them like a fairy palace. Blue lights were moving around its thread-like roads and distant sirens wailed up to them. The red aircraft-warning light of the power station gleamed across the scene, a couple of kilometres to the east. It looked as if it was lower than this balcony. Matt felt for his phone.

'Na-ha-ha-ah!' Liam said and Tyler held up Matt's mobile. 'You might get it back if you make the birds do a little dance for me,' Liam went on, shoving his chest hard against the metal railing at the balcony's edge. He pulled Matt's arm viciously behind his back. The others hemmed in close, ready to back up the boss if there was resistance. There was a glitter of fear in Ahmed's eyes.

'Come on,' breathed Liam with a waft of lager and chilli sauce, and Matt began to understand how his enemies had spent their days excluded from school. 'Bring me some birds. If you don't, the phone goes over first . . .' Tyler dangled Matt's mobile out over the railings. 'Then . . . if you *still* don't. You go over.'

Matt closed his eyes and weighed up his options. Now really would be a good time to ask for help. But what would it cost his bird friends? The oxygen levels were dropping all the time—he could feel it in his fuzzy head and his aching chest; see it in the faces of Ahmed and Tyler, although Liam so far seemed immune. If he didn't get help, and get away from these chimps, he couldn't let Carra know where Morto was; where he was planning to set the seeds free. Because there was no doubt in his mind now. Morto was bringing up flowers in the lift. Why else would he be doing that?

When they'd talked about high points around Thornleigh they'd all thought about hills—trees—the quarry cliff face.

They'd never once thought about the tower block which dominated the town's roughest estate. All the creatures who *had* been able and willing to help would have been following the Night Speakers' instincts. The hills, the trees . . . not this stack of concrete and glass.

Morto had got himself a flat here. Probably months ago. This had always been his plan.

'All right, Bird Boy!' said Liam. 'Say bye-bye to your phone!'

Tyler let the mobile drop. It went silently, flashing up a twinkly farewell from its screen as it tumbled down, spinning. Matt didn't hear it land but he saw a few glints as it exploded and shards flew in all directions.

'Now.' Liam hauled Matt up across the rail until its metal edge grazed his belly. Matt fought back but he felt the blade again, right on his jugular vein, and Tyler pressing in on the other side.

'Guys,' murmured Ahmed, coughing again. 'C'mon! Just . . . y'know . . . scare him . . . yeah?'

'Show me!' insisted Liam, his mouth right against Matt's ear. 'Show me the bird thing! And remember—if I get one single peck off any of them, you're going over.'

When it came, none of them were prepared. Not at all. They were looking out straight across the valley. They had no clue about the way raptors worked; the element of surprise. The buzzard hit Liam from above. How it had got so high when there were no thermals to help it, Matt could only guess, but it must have flown a good thirty metres up above Garramer Towers to get that much velocity.

Over a kilo of bird, travelling at around 100 miles per hour, struck Liam right in the centre of his skull. It laid him out cold on the concrete floor of the balcony. A second buzzard struck Tyler a moment later, toppling him with similar efficiency. Then four or five red kites came for Ahmed, swooping down in a corkscrew of balletic precision. Ahmed stumbled backwards, screaming, coughing, choking. Matt felt the smallest pang. Ahmed had once been his closest friend. Ahmed turned to run, forgot the glass door had been closed, and headbutted it at speed; he rebounded off the unforgiving glass as physics flung him in reverse towards Matt, the back of his skull impacting with the front of Matt's.

Matt felt a bullet of blood crash up through his nose and throat and then, amid a flock of helpful raptors, sank to the floor and lost consciousness across Tyler's legs. The last thing he saw was the upturned face of a worried buzzard.

CHAPTER 44

There were times when Carra wished she had a different job. Getting her Intergalactic Marshal belt two Targan-years ago had been a dream come true, and tracking down criminals on foreign planets had been exciting, scary, a little mind-blowing and always, at the end, incredibly satisfying. She had so far brought thirty-two planet-hopping criminals to justice and her family was immensely proud of her.

But as she rolled the car to a halt on a hill overlooking the small town of Thornleigh, she wished she'd stayed at home on Targa and learnt to cook carraclava for helm parties or drive scouts for tourists visiting the green mountains. Maybe become partnered with a Targan male and had kids.

All this she was most likely never going to do. It looked very much like her planet-hopping was going to end here, on Earth, tonight, in a ball of flame. She had already filed a report and sent it back to the Quorat, detailing everything she had discovered, her plan of action, and the likely outcome. She'd added messages of love for her family too, strictly only to be passed along when news of her death was confirmed.

It was now well past midnight and the wind was getting stronger with every passing minute. She had failed to find Morto. Bringing Targan gadgets through a cleftonique corridor often gave them glitches and she knew her broad-range tracker wasn't working properly. It hadn't worked for nearly a week, since she'd first arrived. If it *had* or if she'd been able to fix it, she would have located Morto probably within a day, and captured him and got out of here without ever messing with the locals. Although she was glad she'd messed with Tima, Elena, and Matt. To discover kids whose brains had been altered by a cleftonique bi-post beam . . . that was news! What they could do with language and animal connection was amazing; she'd fed that information back to the Quorat too.

But it was a one-way message while you were on a planet. Only at the cleftonique post could she get a reply, and not always then.

It gave her some small comfort that she would have added a little bit to the sum of the Quorat's vast knowledge. And that they would think well of her for what she was getting ready to do. Soon. She closed her eyes for a moment, wishing desperately that Morto would materialize on the hillside in front of her, laying out his flowers and his terrible plan, awaiting the perfect point of low pressure. She would step up, collar him, stop him.

And save the lives of everyone in this small town . . . and most of the rest of England.

But when she opened her eyes she didn't see Morto.

She saw Spin.

'I know where he is,' said Spin.

Carra screamed a Targan word which needed no transchip for the boy to understand. She flung the passenger door open and yelled: 'HOW?'

'Well, here's the thing. I broke into the school, went through its records, and found his *address*,' said Spin. 'Old-fashioned, I know.'

'Wait!' Carra paused in putting the key in the ignition. 'His address? What makes you think he's at *home*? This is the kind of place he'll be now—somewhere high up, setting up his poisonous plants so the seed pods can explode and get into the high winds—the jet stream—and terraform the whole planet.'

'Oh—so *that's* it,' the boy replied, infuriatingly cool. 'OK— yes—I can see how that would work. He's at home, I guarantee it.'

'How do you guarantee it?'

'Because his home is as high as this hill. Why would he bother going anywhere else?'

'Direct me!' yelled Carra.

'Wait,' said Spin. 'We pick up Elena first. And Tima.'

'What?! There's no time!'

Spin looked at his watch—an old-fashioned thing with a black leather strap. 'If it's high winds he's after, they're set to peak around 2 a.m. It's nearly one now so that gives us plenty of time.'

'Why do we need them? We know where he is!' snapped Carra.

'Well, let's see. The *superpowers* . . . ?'

Carra paused for moment and then gunned the engine. 'Fair enough,' she said. 'Let's go.'

CHAPTER 45

Hours had passed when Matt finally came to. He was gently pecked awake by a familiar beak. He pushed himself up off Tyler's legs and stared around, aching and dazed. He was on a balcony, in a high wind, surrounded by bodies.

The raptors had departed and Lucky was here, ready to help. He felt a rush of love for her—and then a rush of hopelessness. It might all be too late. The seeds might already be high on the wind, travelling around the country and beyond.

His attackers were still out cold. He felt for Ahmed's pulse first and found it was steady. Next he checked Tyler and Liam. They were not dead. He shoved Ahmed into the recovery position and then, after a pause, did the same for the other two. Tyler groaned and Ahmed coughed. Liam seemed to be snoring. Whatever. Matt was out of here. He had somewhere to be.

He pulled the glass door open with difficulty, what with the bodies, and made his way back through the smelly flat. He shut the front door behind him and stared around the bleak, concrete lift lobby. He was on floor fifteen and the tower had twenty floors. They'd said Mr Janssen—or *Morto*—was on the top floor.

He called the lift, taking long slow breaths to steady himself. There was a painful bump on his forehead and he was getting bouts of dizziness. How much of that was concussion? And how much was bad mist?

'Are you OK, Lucky?' he asked, as he took her into the lift with him.

'OK,' she said. He sensed she was weakened but she was in better shape than he was.

The lift rose up to the top floor and slid open with a chime. He stepped out into an identical lobby and paused, gazing around at the doors to six different flats as the wind howled weirdly up through the lift shaft. Which flat was Morto in?

He was about to start working his way around all the buzzers when he spotted a dark corner on the far side of a jutting wall which enclosed the lift shaft. Beyond the corner was a ladder, reaching up to an access hatch in the ceiling. The hatch was open.

It made perfect sense. The gale was approaching its maximum rage. And Morto and his plants were on the roof.

CHAPTER 46

There was a tapping on the window. Elena sat up, blinking. She'd been deeply asleep alongside Mum. Had she dreamt it?

Tap tap tap. She realized the sound wasn't coming from her mum's window—it was her own. Mum slept on as she slipped out, collecting her bag and trainers and padding across the landing to her bedroom. It was just gone 1 a.m. Soon the beam would have come through and woken her—probably for the last time. Who was tapping? Matt? Tima? Carra?

She pulled back her curtains and stifled a scream. A vampire was floating outside her window.

She stepped back, catching her breath, and then pushed it slightly open to hiss: 'Spin! What the hell?'

'Let me in,' he said, kneeling on the outer sill, his black coat flapping wildly behind him.

'No way! You don't get invited in.'

'Ha! Well, I'm coming in anyway.'

'You know that's not allowed!' she hissed.

'Oh—I'm allowed,' he said, pulling the window further open. 'It's not *your* house—it's your mother's. And she likes me.'

Elena felt her jaw drop.

'Didn't you get her message?' asked Spin, landing on her carpet, the wind gusting in behind him. 'She left you a voicemail, with useful information from me.'

Elena continued to stare.

'Oh, seriously, there's not time. Come on, wonderful daughter. We have to go.'

'I'm not going *anywhere* with you,' she said.

'Fine—we'll go without you,' he shrugged. And he went back out through the window. That was when Elena saw Carra in the Land Rover, Tima waving agitatedly from the back window.

A minute later she was in the back seat, her skull whacking into the headrest as Carra pulled away with maximum G-force. 'We know where he is!' said Tima. 'We're going there now.'

Elena blinked and shook her head. Tima patted her hand. 'Yeah, I know—Spin at your window is a real mind-bender. Stuff of nightmares.'

'Where are we going?' Elena demanded.

'Garramer Towers,' yelled back Carra. 'Tallest place in town.'

'He's not up in the hills?!'

'No—he's at home,' said Tima. 'He *lives* in the tallest place in town! Why didn't we think to find out where he lived?!'

'Where's Matt?' asked Elena. 'He should be with us.'

'I've called him loads of times,' said Tima. 'It just goes straight to voicemail. I've left loads of messages. He might still be at the hospital.'

'I wish he was here,' said Elena. 'All three of us, like last time.'

'Well, thanks a bunch,' said Spin from the front seat. 'I don't know why I bother.'

'Morto's van full of death-orchids broke down right outside Spin's place,' explained Tima.

Elena rubbed her face. She had never imagined Spin having a 'place'. A crypt, maybe.

'So Spin hears Morto calling this mechanic and the mechanic shows up later and asks about what's in the van— Morto tells him it's flowers. Then the mechanic starts talking about the fire at the school garden and Morto freaks out, asks if a woman was there, then punches him to the ground and drives off without paying. So Spin puts two and two together and goes and breaks in to Harcourt High and finds the gardener's address. Then he somehow finds Carra and . . . well . . . here we are.'

'I would have told all that *much* better,' said Spin.

'I can probably do this on my own,' said Carra, cornering much more expertly than she had a few hours back. 'But it may help to have you along. With your . . . talents. We'll call by Matt's place just in case he's there.'

'How long have we got?' Elena checked her watch. It was 1.26 a.m. She really hoped Matt was home. They skidded to a halt outside the car wash at 1.33 a.m. The flat was in darkness.

Tima and Elena waited while Spin first knocked on the door and then somehow flung himself up on to the canopy and ran lightly across to Matt's window.

For a few seconds the world went away for Elena. And for Tima. At 1.34 a.m. the beam came through. They both took a swift breath and closed their eyes. Elena felt tears welling up. There was nothing more beautiful and serene than those few golden seconds when the beam passed by—and this could be the last time.

Spin clunked back into the front passenger seat. 'He's not there. Good! Let's go.'

'You were really out of order last night,' said Elena, as Carra drove on into the estate. She didn't look at Spin as she said it. She was sick with fear, yet still making room for anger at Spin.

'He wants revenge,' warned Tima. 'He said he's going to kill you.'

'Yeah, well, that's fine,' said Spin. 'I'll be delighted to let him try. If we survive the next hour.'

CHAPTER 47

Matt nearly couldn't make the climb. The ladder was vertical, bolted to the wall, and he was so tired. His head spun as he reached the halfway point and it was only Lucky, fluttering up above him, that brought him back out of it. He took a long slow breath and then forced his heavy limbs to obey. The hatch was open; night air gusting down through it. It should have been refreshing but it wasn't.

It was thin.

He staggered out on to the roof of the tower block and groaned with horror. The roof was huge—big enough to cover the dimensions of six spacious council flats. It should have been open to the elements but most of it was covered in a taut, transparent canopy of plastic, stretched flat across the tops of the high perimeter walls. The whole roof had been turned into a massive greenhouse. Apart from some aerials, a small maintenance hut, and a massive water tank with a red aircraft-warning light on top, every part of it was filled with harandelas. Some of them were in pots but most of them were planted in soil; Morto had made an actual garden. There were *thousands* of plants here. Matt realized the nursery at school was just a tiny fraction of what Morto had grown—maybe as a back-up in case his roof garden was discovered.

'So—what do you think?'

Matt spun around to find Mr Janssen—a.k.a. Morto—standing calmly beside the water tank, holding a long blade.

'It's beautiful, isn't it?' said Morto. 'My perfect plants. My life's work.'

'They are beautiful,' agreed Matt. 'But they nearly killed my mum and dad. They *have* killed at least seven people.'

Morto shrugged and waved the blade airily. 'Seven. Seven hundred. It won't matter soon.'

'You're poisoning our whole planet,' stated Matt. He realized part of him was hoping the man would laugh and tell him that this was ridiculous. That this would turn out to be a crazy misunderstanding. That only a few people were affected by being close to his plants and it could all be sorted out.

But Morto just nodded and said: 'How did you find out?'

Matt shook his head, another wave of dizziness assailing him. He was in the thick of a small *forest* of harandelas now. There couldn't be much oxygen left. 'We spoke to a marshal—Carra,' he burbled. 'She's coming to get you. You're . . . you're history, Morto.'

Morto laughed and said: 'Good night, Matteus. Sleep well.'

Matt slid down among the cool, green stems and felt his mind cloud over. His face was next to one of those little domes—a seed pod—swaying in the wind, whistling through the gaps in the plastic, and nudging against his bruised forehead. He could *hear* it crackling and hissing. Getting ready to burst. 'Lucky,' he murmured. 'Get . . . away.' But Lucky was right there, her wing against his cheek, going nowhere. Did he have any more Night Speaker cards to play? He'd probably played his last hand against Liam and the others; the buzzard and kites would be exhausted; maybe even dead.

He heard a tearing sound and saw Morto was reaching up and slicing the plastic canopy open, letting strips of it fly wildly in the wind. 'Nearly time!' he yelled, cheerfully.

CHAPTER 48

Tima felt the first thrum of energy as Carra was gadget-busting the electrical lock on the ground floor of Garramer Towers. 'Something's changed,' she said.

Elena looked around at her. 'What? What's changed.'

'It's . . . clearing,' said Tima. She couldn't explain any further because it was time to run for the lift. They jumped in as soon as it arrived and punched the button for floor twenty.

Carra was consulting her short-range tracer as the lift rose at speed, whining urgently as if it was on their side. 'He's here. Spin was right.'

Spin wasn't in the lift with them. He had opted for the stairs, flying up the first set, coat flapping behind him, and vanishing from sight. 'Nasty light,' was all he'd said as he left them. Tima checked her watch under the flickering fluorescent strip. If the weather forecast was right, the heaviest of the low pressure was moving across Thornleigh right now.

The lift door opened and they poured out into the top-floor lobby. 'There!' yelled Carra, and ran to a set of steps leading up to a hatch in the roof.

When they arrived up on top, a titanic squid was flapping its tendrils across the sky. Tima felt a leap of darkly familiar horror before she realized they were looking at long runners of plastic, sliced away from a fine wire frame, flickering madly in the high wind. Beneath the plastic streamers lay *thousands* of harandelas. She could almost *hear* the tension on the stems as each prepared to explode its seeds into the atmosphere.

Carra did not stop to stare. She ran along a narrow path to the far side of the roof, where a tall man was busy ripping more strips of plastic off the frame. Elena, meanwhile, dropped to her knees with a cry. 'MATT! Tima—it's MATT!' Tima saw their friend lying among the green stems, his eyes shut, Lucky pressed close against his cheek.

'We need help!' cried Elena, a sob in her voice. 'We're supposed to be doing something. We're supposed to be *Night Speaking*, but there's not enough oxygen . . . we can't call them. They can't come.'

Tima saw Carra leap towards the man with the blade and sparks began to fly. Literally. She had some kind of weapon which was fizzing like a sparkler and he was holding her off with that blade. He was laughing and shouting: 'Too late, marshal! Way too late!'

Tima stared across at the duel. What could she do?

Getting into a fight between two warring aliens probably wasn't going to help anyone. But now, if her instincts weren't fooling her, it looked like there was something else she could try. Something . . .

A huge gust of wind woke Matt. He sat up suddenly, nearly headbutting Elena and sending Lucky flapping upwards. 'Where is he?!'

'Carra's fighting him,' said Elena. 'But it might be too late—listen.'

Matt could hear it too. That crackling, straining sound. The seed pods about to blow. And now the plastic awning was rippling crazily above them in strips; there was no way they could stop the seeds from travelling.

'She thinks she can stop it if she can stop *him*,' said Matt. 'So we have to help her do that.'

He staggered to his feet and felt the wind blow some of his dizziness away. 'Aliens! Trouble incoming!' he yelled, grabbing Elena's arm. They ran to the edge of the roof where Carra and Morto were flinging insults, metal, and sparks at each other.

'Help,' Lucky squawked after them. 'Incoming!'

Tima watched her friends run into the action and turned away. She ran for the water tower instead. There was a ladder bolted to it and she climbed it fast, finding herself on a flat iron square with no railings. Now probably wasn't the time to look down. She had a little bit of sky space above her—the flapping, plastic streamers were at knee-level here. She turned her face away from the tearing gusts and closed her eyes. If she was right, the wind that might be their doom might also be the wind that saved them.

Down in the basin valley of Thornleigh and in all the woodlands and grasslands around it, the air was being whipped up, pushed around, swirled up and down and along and through. After days of stillness the thin atmosphere was being shaken like a flat pillow and plumped up with fresh air. Fresh *oxygen*. New energy was coursing through the wildlife. Their friends were reviving. Tima called to mind the insects she needed most, praying she wasn't wrong about them, and sent out a plea. *Please come. I don't know if you'll survive this but please come. Without you we'll all die.*

Carra's sparkling weapon was thrown into the sky and Morto pinned her down easily. 'What now, marshal?' he said, grinning.

Matt leapt on to the man's back but was thrown off immediately and smashed against the concrete wall that ran around the perimeter of the roof. Carra's weapon landed somewhere in the plants and stopped sparkling. If she could get it, Elena thought, she might be able to activate it. But as the plants swayed wildly in the wind she had no idea where to find it. The rats, though, did. A torrent of sleek, furry rodents began to flow past her ankles, showing her the way. That they could move and breathe—let alone *help* was amazing to her. But something was changing. Tima was right. It was *clearing*.

Elena seized the weapon—a baton with a ridged handle and a slider switch below the thumb; it reminded her of her cousin's toy lightsabre. She ran back through the plants, pressing the slider. At once the sparkler mode was back, thrumming with hot energy. Morto was aiming his blade at Carra, pinning her down by the throat with his free hand while she writhed like a serpent. Elena swiped the weapon into his shoulder and, with both horror and triumph, saw it slice right through to the bone.

Morto screamed and flipped around to come for Elena. She stumbled backwards, dropping the sparkler blade and then scrabbling for it. But Morto found it first. He held it with great assurance, smiling down at her as he lifted it above his head, oblivious to the blood pouring from his wounded shoulder. His aim, as he brought it down toward her face, would have been perfect . . . but for the bats flying into his face.

He yelled, missing Elena by a hair's breadth, and then swiped the fragile, winged creatures away from him.

Carra, meanwhile, had scrambled to her feet and was back in the fight, pulling out another weapon. It looked like the gun she'd shot Spin and Tima with. But Morto, even badly wounded, was faster still. He launched himself at her, slicing the blade into her left arm and pistoning the sparkler baton towards her face. Carra flinched backwards with a shriek of pain and stumbled across the waist-height wall.

Elena screamed and a torrent of rats rushed to help, but they were too small and too late.

From her vantage point on top of the water tower, Tima saw several virtually impossible things happen. First, Carra teetered on the edge of the wall, see-sawing between life and death while Morto grabbed her knees and prepared to tip her over.

Next, a glittering cloud passed over them all and dropped like rain. Then a vampire leapt out of nowhere and landed on Morto, sinking his fangs into the back of the alien's neck. Morto swung around, letting Carra drop back on to the roof, and threw Spin into the plants before turning back and grabbing Carra again, seizing her and hauling her upwards, ready to throw . . .

Meanwhile Matt had staggered to his feet and was staring into the sky, lifting both hands and waving as if he was doing some kind of runway air-traffic control.

Finally, a golden eagle landed, screeching, on Morto's head, and drove its talons in.

CHAPTER 49

Morto's cries of pain were chilling. The golden eagle perched on his head flapped its massive two-metre wingspan for balance. Blood dripped from the puncture wounds where its talons still held and its viciously curved beak hovered low over Morto's brow, ready to take out his eyes. Carra grabbed the backpack she'd dumped nearby on the floor. Reaching into it she unleashed a small, blue ball of lightning which looped around her enemy's writhing form, rendering him utterly still.

As the eagle continued to roost on his head, letting out an occasional warning hiss, Carra checked in all his pockets and pulled out a square-screened gadget. 'Code,' she said.

Morto groaned.

'Code,' repeated Carra. 'Or Matt will have his friend puncture your eyeballs one at a time.'

Matt stood next to her. 'That's just what I was thinking,' he said.

Morto groaned again and spat out a series of numbers. Carra tapped them in.

'Hand,' she said, and the blue lines released his arm long enough for him to place a palm print on the screen.'

Carra swirled through the displays and found a map, covered in glowing red dots. She looked up at Morto and smiled. 'We've torched all your spares,' she said. 'This is all you have left.'

She waved the screen at Matt and Elena. 'It's his plant bio-tracker. Everything he has created. What's left is all up here. Morto,' she said. 'I know your work. You always build in a bio failsafe. You can disintegrate these right up to the last moment. If you don't activate that in three seconds, I will torch everything on this roof—you included. If you *do*, I will make it safe, arrest you, take you back to the Quorat, and prosecute you. Ayot will bring in its best legal people and there's a chance you might get some of your life back one day.'

Morto began to laugh. The eagle screeched and Morto joined it. And then he spluttered: 'There *is* no bio failsafe for this! Failure was never an option. I can't stop it. The seeds are going to fly around this planet and there's nothing you can do.'

The wind picked up to a howling gale at just that point and Tima, still up on the water tank, saw Carra's face set like a steel mask. She turned back to her bag and withdrew the silver pyramid, placing it on the ground and pressing its tip.

'Wait!' yelled Matt. 'He's lying!'

'He isn't,' sighed Carra, as the bubble formed around the

259

tower roof and then expanded to take in at least a kilometre around the whole building.

'What are you doing?' yelled Elena. 'You can't torch us! You can't torch everyone in this bubble! That's hundreds . . . thousands of people!'

'It's better than I thought,' said Carra, sadly. 'I thought I would have to burn most of England, remember. Now I've seen his bio-tracker I know it's just here. But I have to be sure.'

'But . . . you'll die,' said Elena, running to her and grabbing her hands. 'We'll all die!'

'Everybody dies eventually,' said Carra. 'I'm sorry—I wish I could set you all free but there's no time. Listen . . . they're going to burst! You can *hear* it. They're fizzing . . . they're just about to blow.'

'Erm, actually . . .' Spin got up from amid the plants where Morto had thrown him. 'I don't think they are.' He held up a harandela plant and it sagged in his hands. The flower was OK but the stem was collapsing under the weight of fifty or sixty insects.

'Locusts,' called Tima, from up on the water tank. 'Didn't you notice them arrive?'

'Well, she *was* fighting for her life,' pointed out Spin. 'That kind of thing can be distracting.'

Carra stared around her, gaping. Above the howling of the wind and the flapping of the plastic strips rose a fizzing, crackling sound. The carpet of harandela plants was slowly collapsing under the weight of a plague of locusts. The mass of insects glittered in the red glow of the aircraft-warning light.

Tima thought she had never seen anything so beautiful.

'They've eaten the seed pods,' she said. 'They did that first. And now they're eating the rest of the plant. If this isn't enough . . . I mean if you think that locust droppings will still manage to spread those alien seeds . . . you'd better go ahead and torch us all.'

Carra shook her head slowly. 'How did you do this? I thought . . . I thought the animals were too weak. Poisoned by the bad air.'

'They were,' said Tima. 'But then the wind came. It blew out the old, stale air and brought in the fresh stuff. I mean . . . we were all up on the roof and surrounded by these things and we should have been choking . . . but the wind saved us.'

'*You* saved us,' said Carra. 'And them.' She sank down against the wall she'd so nearly been tipped over and wiped her hands across her face.

'I called for help hours ago and then I stopped because I knew they couldn't do anything,' said Tima, pretty dazed herself. 'I thought they'd just stopped too. But they hadn't. My insects! They *knew* what was needed. All of them. They brought the locusts here. I mean . . . where are locusts even *from*? We don't get them in England! But here they are . . .'

'So . . .' Elena knelt down next to Carra. 'Is this enough? Is it over? Or do you still have to . . . ?'

'We'll wait,' said Carra. 'We'll wait until dawn so I can see properly. Seeds eaten by locusts aren't seeds any more. The plants can't grow again. But I need to see all this with my own eyes.'

They clustered together along the wall, sheltering from the

261

wind as it slowly died down. Tima cuddled against Elena and Matt leant, exhaustedly, on her other shoulder. 'What happened to your face?' she said. 'Did Morto beat you up before we got here?'

'Nah,' said Matt. 'That was just a headbutt from my old mate. To be fair, he *was* being taken out by red kites at the time.'

Elena sighed. 'Tell me later. My brain can't take any more.'

She got her first aid kit out and went to bandage Carra's bleeding arm.

Spin was staring at the immobilized body of Morto; the glowing blue tape now also across his mouth to silence him and the eagle still sat on his head. Then he glanced over at Carra, as Elena worked on her wound. 'Um . . . about this staying here until dawn thing . . .'

'Yeah—it's all set to be a bright, sunny morning,' growled Matt. 'You're going to love it, Dracula.'

CHAPTER 50

The string section swelled, Tima held Lily's hand, opened up her throat, and sang out the sweetest soprano she could produce. She sang about a winding river, its bank covered with flowers. Alongside her, Lily did the same—their voices entwining in harmony.

The audience was spellbound; holding its breath as the duet rose and fell and spiralled like birdsong, supported by the most talented musicians Mr James had been able to find; past and present music students from Prince William Prep. As the duet reached its crescendo, Tima felt shivers of delight sweeping across her skin. To be able to make such a sound . . . even with her school enemy . . . was pretty special.

As they reached their final, long, sweet notes, an avalanche of flowers dropped on to the stage.

In the audience, Elena and Matt screamed. Just a little.

For a few seconds, those blooms really did look *just like* harandelas.

But the harvest festival concert had only Earth plants, fruit, and vegetables on display. There were no harandelas left. They'd seen to that. Tima's locusts had reduced Morto's crop to just a few spindly sticks by the time dawn had come, eight days ago. They didn't seem to be bothered by the toxicity which had disintegrated Tima's bee friends and slowed down the native insects. Locusts were, after all, some of the hardiest insects on the planet.

Convinced, Carra had deactivated the dome and let the swarm go—and it had risen up, a dark cloud, and flown away back to southern Europe or Asia or wherever it had miraculously flown in from.

The only creature more keen to fly away had been Spin. As dawn approached he had pulled up his cowl and huddled in the shadow of the water tank. He and Matt hadn't spoken through the rest of that night and Elena knew it would be a long time before they'd ever reach a truce. Which was a shame because she was pretty sure there was a lot of good stuff in Spin . . . if only he could be persuaded to stop creeping around in the dark and biting people. She hadn't seen him since that morning.

The people of Thornleigh had recovered remarkably quickly. There had been a few deaths but the victims did not include Mr James or Lily's mum. Or Mr Rosen who, it emerged, had collapsed and been taken home earlier on the day of the fire in the greenhouse. They had all now fully recovered and the spontaneous combustion of their rare flowers was simply a mystery they'd never solve. No gas had been found escaping the town's power plant and although there *was* some social media chatter about toxic plants in the area, no such plants had been traced. Matt's outburst at the hospital never made it on to TV.

Elena and Matt met Tima after the concert, fighting their way through crowds of people who wanted to tell her—and Lily—how marvellous they were.

'We rehearsed for *ages!*' Lily was saying, stridently. 'Tima came over to my house, as soon as Mum was better, and I helped her with her French pronunciation.'

Tima glanced at Matt and Elena and rolled her eyes a little.

'But Tima helped *me* with my breathing control,' went on Lily, and Tima blinked in surprise and grinned.

'I'm quite good at breathing,' said Tima. 'It goes "in-out-in-out".' The crowd around them laughed.

'See you later, Tee!' called out Elena, reaching over to pat her friend's head.

'Usual time and place,' added Matt.

They headed home, leaving Tima to her admirers. They'd tell her what *they* thought of her performance—and that *hilarious* flower-dropping moment—when they all met up at the den tonight.

Matt walked Elena home and they stared up at the stars quite a lot.

'Which one do you think Carra's on?' asked Elena.

Matt shrugged. 'Dunno. It's weird to think about, isn't it? I wish we'd had more time to talk.'

'Well, she had a prisoner to escort,' said Elena. Carra had sent them all home minutes after the harandelas were confirmed dead, tolerating goodbye hugs from Elena and Tima—and even from Matt. Spin, though, hadn't said goodbye. He had vanished the moment the dome was lifted, breathing hard, obviously in pain.

'I think we'll see her again,' added Elena. 'She's got that corridor thing, hasn't she? I bet she'll come back one day. How's your dad now?'

'He's up out of bed,' said Matt. 'Mum seems fine but he's still got a cough. He wasn't that healthy to start with. More car-wash action for me, of course.' He shrugged tiredly. 'Got to keep the family business going.'

'You know Liam's back at school tomorrow, don't you?' she said.

'Yep,' said Matt. 'And Tyler and Ahmed.'

'Are you going to tell anyone about how they attacked you?'

'Nope.'

'Do you really think they'll leave you alone now? After what happened with the birds?'

'What birds?' Matt grinned and called Lucky down from a nearby lamp post. 'Liam didn't see a thing,' he said, as the starling landed on his wrist. 'Nor did Tyler. Ahmed did . . . he saw quite a lot.'

'Oh dear,' sighed Elena.

'No—it's good. I think he might stay away from Liam from now on. Now he knows how close he came to being mates with a potential murderer.'

Matt and Lucky peeled off once they reached the end of Elena's street and she went on to her door alone.

Mum was asleep already by the time she got in, so she made herself some tea and buttered toast and sat down at the kitchen table to eat it. The silence was comforting.

Tap tap tap.

She jumped violently and slammed down her mug.

'What the hell?'

A pale face loomed beyond the glass. She opened the door to the garden and peered out. 'Why do you have to be so creepy, Spin?'

'It comes with the job,' he said, sidling past her into the kitchen. 'Is your lovely mum still up?'

'Don't *call* her that!' said Elena.

'Why not? She's very lovely. As mums go.' He sat down and helped himself to a slice of toast. 'What's she got?'

'What do you mean?' Elena folded her arms and glared at him.

'She takes loads of pills,' he said. 'She was knocking them back with her tea.'

'She's got bipolar disorder, if you must know. Why are you here? And remember . . . I *can* uninvite you.'

'Not staying long, just thought I'd check in. Wanted to know how everyone is.'

Elena leant against the fridge and folded her arms. There was a vampire in her kitchen. Could she *ever* get a few hours' pass from weirdness? 'Since when did you ever care about how everyone is?'

He swallowed and licked some butter off his black-taloned fingers. 'You know me so well. No . . . I just came to tell you . . . I'll be away for a while.'

'Where are you going?'

'Not important,' he said, standing up. 'Just . . . won't be out at night for a bit. Just thought you should know, in case you need any rescuing again. You won't find me.'

'You didn't rescue me!' she said.

'Well, that's the thanks I get for working out who Morto was and taking you and Tima to the tower block in the nick of time, when you would have just slept on to your doom. No. No really, don't thank me!' He backed away to the door.

She gave a sigh, raised her hands, and then dropped them. 'OK. You did well. Thanks.'

He smiled and then stared down at the floor for a while. 'Send me happy thoughts,' he said. 'I'll see you in a while.'

And he vanished into the dark.

Elena followed him out into the garden. He was already gone, though, as suddenly as he always arrived. She went back in the house to get something and, sitting on the edge of the patio, turned it over in her hands. She shivered. Winter was on its way.

A furry warmth stole across her left arm and she smiled, delighted. 'Hello Velma.' The vixen settled against her and let out a short sigh, sending a curl of breath vapour out in the light from the kitchen.

Being a Night Speaker was amazing and often terrifying— but at this moment a beautiful wild animal was choosing to sit here and warm her from skin to heart. And that was the best bit.

She looked up into the sky and then at the black stick with the green button. *How to contact Carra.*

Her finger rested on the button. Maybe tonight . . . ? Maybe tomorrow . . . ? Maybe in a crisis. Maybe never . . .

ACKNOWLEDGEMENTS

Grateful thanks for botanical guidance from Bryan Greenwood and Andy McIndoe. Who knew the difference between pollinating and splicing, Bryan? You. Not me. Also to Sam Taylor and Clare Taylor for their knowledge and experience on the Spin front.

And to Liz Cross for slashing those three superfluous chapters like a literary Boudicca and Deborah Sims for all the gentle nudges about the twiddly bits.

Ali Sparkes was a journalist and BBC broadcaster until she chucked in the safe job to go dangerously freelance and try her hand at writing comedy scripts. Her first venture was as a comedy columnist on *Woman's Hour* and later on *Home Truths*. Not long after, she discovered her real love was writing children's fiction.

Ali grew up adoring adventure stories about kids who mess about in the woods and still likes to mess about in the woods herself whenever possible. She lives with her husband and two sons in Southampton, England.

WANT TO KNOW WHERE THE STORY BEGAN? READ ON FOR A TASTE OF NIGHT SPEAKERS

CHAPTER 1

Elena woke up at 1.34 a.m. She didn't need to check the alarm clock on the bedside table. She knew it was 1.34 a.m. It was always 1.34 a.m.

This was the seventh night in a row, and it was getting to be almost normal.

She prodded the button on the clock anyway, and its dim blue light showed **1.34** in blocky digital numbers across the glass. 'Hello again, one thirty-four,' she mumbled. She got up. There was no point staying in bed and trying to get back to sleep; this she had also learned over the past week.

She opened her door without making a sound and slipped downstairs to the kitchen. Since night three she had been getting a hot drink and taking it back up to her room with a couple of biscuits. Then she would sit by her window and consume them, watching the silent, shadowy street below. It was reassuring somehow—making a normal routine out of something so weird.

The first night was nothing that strange, of course. Everyone got insomnia once in a while, didn't they? She had woken up at 1.34 a.m and then been unable to get back to sleep until around six. By breakfast she was groggy but not too tired for school. She hadn't even mentioned it to Mum.

The next night was when it started to get weird. Her eyes pinged open at 1.34 a.m. again. Even then, she wasn't sure it was the same time; the exact same time, to the minute. She really only noticed *that* the third night. But maybe she noticed the song that second night . . . maybe not. It was hard to be sure.

By now, though, sitting at the window on night seven, she knew it all. The time was always 1.34 a.m. exactly and what shoved her so abruptly out of sleep was something like a song. In her dreams there was a long, chiming note like someone sliding a metal spoon down an ancient bell, then a swell of . . . a voice? Was it a voice? It seemed like something singing. A dark and yet somehow golden song that rushed along like a river . . . a thin, straight river . . . a channel of vibrating dark golden song, fizzing and bubbling and beautiful.

'Will you shut up?' she said, out loud. The talking to herself had started on night five. As long as she didn't shout she knew she couldn't be heard. Mum slept like the dead. 'Seriously . . . it's just a sound in your head. Like . . . that ear thing . . . tinnitus or something. It's nothing mystical or sinister. And 1.34 a.m. is probably just when some big machine starts up over on the industrial estate. Or at the power station. Something is making a noise and you're hearing it in your sleep and you're waking up. That's all.'

So why can't you still hear it once you're awake? asked the argumentative imp who plagued these nights by the window.

'It's short. It's gone by the time I sit up,' she explained.

OK—and why can't you just drop back off to sleep again?

'I don't know. I'm just stressed, I guess. Early hours waking—that's a classic symptom of anxiety. I know. I looked it up on the internet.'

Seven nights in a row . . . ? REALLY? Do 13-year-olds usually get that stressed? Is this normal?

She'd looked it up online. She'd typed in 'Why do I keep waking up at the same time each night?' A lot of suggestions came back: noisy neighbours, a gas boiler starting up on a timer, hormonal activity, pets, poltergeists, trapped wind . . .

She knew that it was nothing to do with any of the stuff she had read online. It was something else. Something *very* else. Maybe in the morning she would talk to Mum. Maybe. If Mum seemed OK; if she was having a good day.

Elena settled back into her chair and put her bare feet on the windowsill. On the street below a fox trotted along the pavement, pausing to sniff at the wheelie bins. It cast a long shadow under the dim street lights. Elena called it Velma because she thought it was probably a vixen. She'd seen it several times now. Three of those times it had paused and seemed to stare right up at her for a few seconds, before trotting away on its own business.

The terraced houses opposite seemed to stare back at her, their windows like dark, blank eye sockets. She opened her own window and breathed in the night air. It was sweet and cool, full of late May blossom and recently drenched gardens. It had been raining when she'd gone to bed at ten. Clouds drifted across the scattering of stars above, tinged with orange from the distant lights of the industrial estate. The town's street lights were energy-saving blue, but Quarry End remained defiantly lit by tall orange lamps that stayed on all night, fighting off the shadow of the broken hillside that loomed over it. The orange glow seeped across the sky towards the quiet suburban streets where Elena lived, two or three kilometres away.

She picked up a book and settled down at the window to read the night away. A bit of Cathy Cassidy would pass the time, and then she could get into bed with the dawn chorus to sing her to sleep. She might get another hour in before the alarm went off.

Maybe she fell asleep then; maybe she didn't. All she remembered later, in one of those stuttering leaps of time she kept getting, was that her forehead was against the window again, and the night beyond the thin glass seemed to be dissolving through it like tears through tissue.

And standing quite still in the street below was a solitary, misty figure, pointing a gun at her.